BRIDEGROOM
ON LOAN

BY
EMMA RICHMOND

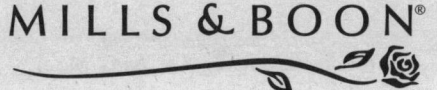

MILLS & BOON®

First published in Great Britain 1999
Harlequin Mills & Boon Limited,
Eton House, 18-24 Paradise Road, Richmond, Surrey TW9 1SR

© Emma Richmond 1999

ISBN 0 263 81693 1

Set in Times Roman 10½ on 12½ pt.
02-9906-39775 C1

Printed and bound in Spain
by Litografía Rosés, S.A., Barcelona

'I'm not free, Carrie.'

'She left you... And I want to kiss you. Do you have *any* idea how much I want to kiss you? I *need* you,' Carrie cried. 'All my life I've waited for someone like you! It can't be wrong! How can it be wrong, Beck?'

Moving towards him, body shaking, she touched her hands to his rigid shoulder.

He watched what she was doing, unmoving, and then he turned his head towards her. He was so close, her mouth a bare inch from his, and his eyes looked as if they were smouldering in the flickering light. She parted her lips as though unable to help it, and so he kissed her. And restraint shattered.

Emma Richmond was born during the war in north Kent when, she says, 'Farms were the norm and motorways non-existent. My childhood was one of warmth and adventure. Amiable and disorganised, I'm married with three daughters, all of whom have fled the nest—probably out of exasperation! The dog stayed, reluctantly. I'm an avid reader, a compulsive writer and a besotted new granny. I love life and my world of dreams, and all I need to make things complete is a housekeeper—like, yesterday!'

Recent titles by the same author:

ONE BRIDE REQUIRED!

CHAPTER ONE

THE M23 was coned off all the way to Gatwick, or had been—the wind was playing absolute havoc with the presumably once tidy contraflow arrangement which forced everyone to drive on the hard shoulder. Everyone? There was only herself and that lunatic lorry driver behind her. Well, if he thought she was going to speed up, he was mistaken. Driving in the dark was bad enough. Driving in the dark on a narrow, coned-off lane with the strong wind nudging the car sideways every few seconds and the lorry's headlights dazzling her was the stuff of nightmares. And if he got any closer he would be in her boot!

Maniac, Carenza muttered to herself. What had happened to knights of the road? Once upon a time drivers had been kind, thoughtful, *helpful.* Not this idiot. As she neared the airport turn-off, the coning ended and the lorry thundered past her with a whoosh of displaced air. Watching his tail-lights disappear, she felt suddenly abandoned, and gave a disgruntled smile. Perverse, Carrie. Very perverse. And if she hadn't forgotten her notebook she wouldn't have *needed* to drive in the dark. Or in a hurricane, which was what it felt like.

Hastily over-correcting as another strong gust punched the side of the car, she was so busy concentrating on keeping straight, she missed the turn-off, and, like a fool, took the next one, stupidly assuming that it would take her back to where she wanted to go. It didn't, and she drove on too long, searching for a familiar sign instead of turning round and going back. But the road must come out *somewhere*.

Calm down, she adjured herself. Relax. Just take it slow. This was West Sussex, not some forgotten outpost, and all roads must eventually lead to a town. Horsham wasn't that far away. Not that anyone would ever have known it, because there were no lights to be seen at all, which seemed crazy when she was in striking distance of at least two motorways and a busy airport.

Turning left at the next junction for the simple reason that it *felt* right, she drove into the forest. Glancing nervously at the trees that surrounded her, trees that were being thrashed into a frenzy, she really did begin to think that she should go home, and ring Beck in the morning. The wind was definitely getting worse. Small branches began to litter the road ahead, swept along in a crazy dance, and the car that always felt so comforting now began to feel very fragile. She remembered all too well the last storm to hit Britain, the damage it had caused, but surely, surely, the weathermen would have been more on their toes this time?

You didn't watch the news, Carenza. And although it had been *windy* when she'd left home it hadn't been anything like this. A bit late now to berate herself for a fool... Her headlights washed over an old building and she hastily braked to a halt. She couldn't tell whether it was empty, or abandoned, but it was certainly closed up. An old pub. The Muted Dragon. And absolutely no help to her at all.

Driving on, she reached a crossroads, and, thankfully, a sign. Horsham was to the right, and so the best thing would be to drive there. She knew her way to Beck's place from Horsham.

Feeling more confident, she picked up speed, passed tall gates with the words Dragon's Rest picked out in gold, and she gave a small smile. What was with the dragons?

A small animal ran across the road in front of her, startling her. A fox maybe, or a rabbit—and then, over and above the noise of the engine and the wind, she heard a roaring, like an express train thundering out of control.

Frightened, she glanced frantically round—and didn't believe what she was seeing. Trees, magnificent old trees that had been standing for hundreds of years, were being toppled like wheat.

And she was right in their path.

Realising that she had eased her foot off the accelerator, she hastily jammed it back down, but it was too late. The roaring became a shriek, as though all the furies of hell were chasing her. Then the tree to her right, just a little way in front of her, didn't merely topple, it was viciously uprooted. She knew that accelerating wouldn't save her, braking wouldn't save her, but she tried anyway.

It hit just behind her head and she frantically threw herself sideways, tucked her upper half into the well of the passenger seat as the giant trunk slowly, and inexorably, crushed the flimsy metal above her.

CHAPTER TWO

BENT in half, eyes screwed shut, arms outstretched, breath held, she waited. She could almost feel the weight of it, almost hear the settling of tortured metal, but not quite. Not above the howling of the wind that was now not only outside the car, but in.

Cautiously opening her eyes, she squinted sideways. From what she could see, which wasn't very much, the tree had crushed the door and the back of the seat and now lay at an angle above her. Not touching her, but an inch or so above her hunched back. The car roof had been crumpled, the windscreen and side windows were gone and glass was showered across her thighs. The odd thing was, she felt quite objective about it all. Not panicky, or hysterical, just objective. She wasn't hurt—at least, she didn't think she was. Cramped, lying awkwardly, but not hurt. It was also like being in a wind tunnel. Dust and grit were whirled about her and she had to squint her eyes shut to avoid damage.

She was an independent girl, used to fending for herself, and it didn't even occur to her that she might wait until someone came along to help.

Cautiously raising her head, she encountered metal, and lowered it again. The gear lever was dig-

9

ging into her hip. She shifted slightly, the car groaned, and she lay still.

The tree was heavy, she told herself, so the car wasn't going anywhere. She also thought that the tree had done all the crushing it was going to do. So...

She tried to lever her feet up on what was left of the driver's seat, and couldn't. Tried to wriggle out from under the crushed metal, and couldn't. Curved over like a bow, face down, she was effectively stuck—unless she could push the seat back.

Her long dark hair hanging over her face, shoulders hunched, she groped under the seat to locate the lever, pulled—and the seat shot back with the force of a rocket. Dumped head-first on the floor, she cursed, then swore as the car alarm went off.

This was silly.

And why was it, she wondered, that the English always considered how they looked before considering how they felt? Weird.

She managed to get her upper half on to the cushion, managed to lower the seat back—and then wondered whether you could actually open a hatchback from the inside. Well, she decided crossly as she struggled to free herself, if she couldn't she would just have to wait until someone came! Which probably wouldn't be until it got light, or the storm blew itself out. Which didn't sound imminent, although that terrifying roaring and shrieking had gone. A tornado? That was how it had seemed in those few jumbled impressions she'd had before the tree struck. Not that she'd ever seen a tornado first hand, only on news reports, and certainly never in England.

'And will you shut up?' she yelled at the car alarm.

She was wearing herself out with the effort to get free, a temper tantrum imminent, when light flickered across her and was gone.

Startled, she flung up her head. 'Hello?' she called.

'Carenza?' A torch was shone in the crushed side window and she twisted towards it.

'Can you see me?' she shouted stupidly.

'I can see you. Are you hurt?'

'No,' she shouted back. 'I'm stuck!'

Beck, she thought in relief, and if there was one person you needed in a crisis it was someone like Beck. His jacket was being whipped and snapped like rigging on a yacht, hair blown every which way as he reached in to remove the ignition key, and the alarm thankfully stopped its strident call.

Moments later, the rear of the car was lifted, the back seats shoved flat, and the car dipped alarmingly as he crawled into the small space.

'Which part of you is stuck?'

'My hips; I don't have enough leverage.' And she was definitely going on a diet when she got out of this.

He put down the torch, grasped her upper arms,

braced his feet, and pulled. One foot against the splintered dashboard, she pushed, ignored the pain of being squashed like a sausage, and eventually came free.

'Let's get out of here.'

'Just let me get my breath…'

'No time.' He sounded terse, urgent, and for once she didn't argue, just allowed him to drag her free. Into mayhem—and another tree that looked in imminent danger of toppling.

He grabbed her arm and dragged her away from danger. Eyes shut to protect them from the whirling dust and debris, fingers clutched into his coat, she stumbled blindly where he led. Speech and coherent thought were impossible; they needed all their energy for walking, or staggering, to safety. Impossible to stand upright, hair almost tugged from its roots by the force of the gale, they could only go in the direction the wind was blowing. She fell twice and was ruthlessly dragged to her feet, but without Beck she would never have managed.

Power lines were down and were shooting blue sparks across the grass. Avoiding them, detouring round so many fallen trees, climbing over those they couldn't, virtually blind in the pitch-darkness, he forced her on, until thankfully, blissfully, they were in the lee of a building. Exhausted from the battle, they remained there a few moments to catch their breath.

'All right?' he shouted.

She nodded against his shoulder.

'Ready?'

She nodded again, and he urged her along the side of the stone wall, then round the corner where the full force of the wind hit them again. Anchoring her against his side, he halted again, fumbled in his pocket for his keys, unlocked the door and thrust her inside. It took all his strength to shut the door behind them, and the transition from violence to calm left her almost uncomprehending.

She found that she was shaking. Untangling her hair with her fingers, she tucked it behind her ears, savoured the ability to breathe normally. She still couldn't see a thing. But she was aware of him beside her. More aware than she had any right to be.

She heard him flick a switch, but nothing happened. He didn't say anything further, and neither did she. He took her arm and led her blindly across the room and into another one. Low burning coals in the fireplace gave some illumination and he steered her towards an armchair.

His shadow was huge, unreal as he bent to toss a log on the fire, stir it into life, and then he said quietly, 'I'll make some coffee.'

'Thank you.' Her voice was as quiet as his.

The wind sounded somehow worse from inside, as though it were angry that its prey had escaped. And I'll huff and I'll puff, she thought tiredly, and I'll blow your house down. Leaning back, jumping nervously at every crash from outside, she stared at the fire. Flames were beginning to lick round the log. Hungry, devouring, but she was alive, safe, and in the house of Andrew Beckford, known to his friends as Beck. Her employer. A man she'd been avoiding for the past few weeks of working for him. Because it was best.

The first time they'd met, last November, she had thought it would be just another job, another client. She hadn't expected to like him. From the little she had known about him—that he was a marine archaeologist, respected mountaineer, explorer, a crewman in one of the Tall Ships Races—she had expected him to be arrogant, condescending, and he hadn't been like that at all. A tall man with steady grey eyes and brown hair, he exuded a quiet confidence. There had also been an air of sadness about him, of hurt, and, like the fool she sometimes was, she'd allowed her heart to rule her head and agreed to work for him. She should have refused, because when she had discovered that he was engaged to the beautiful Helena it was too late.

She could hear the soft movements he made in the kitchen. With no electricity, he must have gas, or an Aga if he was able to boil a kettle, but it was an absent thought.

When he returned carrying two mugs, she turned her head to watch him. He handed her one, and went to stand by the fireplace, staring down into the fire. The flickering shadows curved his face into a mask, made it unfamiliar, stark; only the eyes seemed alive, bright, intelligent.

'Were you coming to see me?' He spoke quietly, gaze still on the fire.

'No, I'd left my notebook at the centre. I tried ringing you...'

'I wasn't there.'

'No. I should have left it until tomorrow, but I needed to check some figures.'

'And being an impatient sort of person...' he murmured.

'Yes. I didn't know a gale was imminent. I didn't see the weather report. I knew March was supposed to be *windy*, but...' She felt awkward. Nervous of being alone with him. 'And then I missed the turning,' she continued with false brightness. 'What's with the dragons?'

'Dragons?'

'Mm. The Muted Dragon, Dragon's Rest. St Maxim's Forest known for them, is it?'

'Oh, I don't know. A local legend, I expect.'

'I should have asked the one I met. If I'd had time, that is. Trees falling on you tend to limit conversation somewhat. Sorry,' she apologised with a wan smile. 'I always ramble when I'm tired. It's been one hell of a day.' And was liable to get worse. Her awareness of him in the intimacy of the darkened room was ten times worse than it normally was. Unable to sit still, she put her coffee on a nearby table and got to her feet. Hands shoved into her jacket pockets, she walked across to the window. 'What were you doing out? Looking for damage?'

'No, I was on my way home. The road was blocked. I left the Land Rover and walked.'

'Lucky for me.'

'Yes.'

Turning, she gave him a small smile that he probably couldn't see in the dark room. 'I loved that car. Stupid, isn't it? I mean, get a life, Carenza...' Tailing off, she returned her attention to the darkened window. All she could see was herself. She was never at a loss for words. Never. And now she couldn't think of one.

'Are you hungry?'

She shook her head. 'I had something earlier.'

'Then if you'll excuse me for a moment, I'd better empty the freezer.'

'Yes, of course.'

When he'd gone, she returned to the chair and picked up her mug. Both hands wrapped round it for warmth, she stared at the fire. Miss No Brain, she scolded herself. All it needed now was for the beauteous Helena to come wafting in. Even an idiot could have sensed the tension between them—not that she thought Helena an idiot—she didn't know her, didn't *want* to know her—but she couldn't have failed to miss the fact that Beck was as aware and tense as she was. Which naturally begged the question, why? If he was in love with Helena, why would he be attracted to herself? Because he was. She knew he was. The pair of them had been as inarticulate as teenagers. And Beck wasn't a man for inarticulateness. He wasn't a shy man.

Resting her mug on her knee, she continued to stare into the fire. Continued to think about him. Speculate. As she had been doing since the first time she met him.

She didn't remember falling asleep, only remembered waking. Opening her eyes, she stared blankly at the fire. It was freshly banked, warm and cosy. A blanket covered her, and the wind had stopped. Silence. Complete and utter silence. Grey light filled the room, and she turned to look at the window. A window framed by expensive curtains. It was raining, she saw.

Allowing her gaze to roam, she pulled a face, partly envious, partly wry. The whole room was expensive. Being an interior designer, she could tell, almost to the last penny, how much it had all cost. Not entirely to her taste with all those small tables holding lamps, too much like something out of a magazine, but tasteful, she supposed. The only thing she really liked was the fire.

She'd never been in the house, never been alone with him. On the few occasions when they had met, it had always been in the centre when other people were present—and she couldn't believe she'd fallen asleep. Too many late nights, she supposed, and a weekend spent chasing clients who owed her money. And the day-to-day tension that she might

see Beck, of course. Who was engaged to Helena.
And women knew, didn't they? When another
woman was attracted to their man?

You can sometimes be very silly, Carenza. Mas-
ochistic even. Yes.

With a deep sigh, a wide yawn, she pushed the
blanket aside. The knees of her tailored trousers
were torn and muddy, her boots caked with God
only knew what. Her jacket was creased. And she
ached. Stretching to ease her cramped muscles, she
went to peer at her reflection in an ornate mirror,
and tried to smile. Something the cat wouldn't have
brought in. Her long hair was tangled, her mascara
smudged. Wetting a finger, she wiped away the
worst of it and then turned away, because there was
absolutely nothing she could do about how she
looked. She didn't even have a comb with her.

Walking into the large kitchen, she halted with
another dented smile. It was also expensively dec-
orated. A blue enamel Aga stood proudly against
one wall; a matching blue hood with a brass rail
hovered protectively above it. The stone flags were
cold beneath her feet. The oak cupboards and units
matched the long table and chairs, the tiles matched
the floor, the walls the curtains. Someone's idea of
a country kitchen. Except it wasn't. She'd been in a
great many country kitchens, and they didn't look
like this. There should be muddy wellington boots,
raincoats, a dog basket... Where did poor Spanner
sleep? Not here, obviously.

There was no sign of Beck, or Helena, but a kettle steamed gently on the Aga. Milk, sugar and coffee had been left on the work surface. Taking a cup from the mock Welsh dresser, she made herself a hot drink and went to stare from the window. The rain was falling heavy and straight. Noisy. Thunder rumbled in the distance, a low, menacing sound, and she spared a thought for the poor clear-up crews who would be working out in this. She could see a lot of the damage from here. White, ugly scars on the trees where branches had been ripped off, those that were left standing, that was. There were scattered bricks across what looked like a dug-up lawn. Perhaps that was the next item for renovation.

Sipping her coffee, lost in her thoughts, she started when she heard the back door open. Turning, heart beating over-fast, she found a faint smile as Beck walked in. Drowned rat wasn't in it. Hair plastered to his head, jacket and jeans soaked through, he gave a small smile back, but his eyes didn't quite meet hers.

'I'm sorry I wasn't here when you woke,' he apologised quietly. 'I just wanted to check for damage.'

'That's all right. How bad is it?'

'Bad. The "front", as it's being called,' he murmured humorously as he shrugged out of his jacket, shook it and draped it over a chair, 'cut a swathe through the south of England about a mile wide. Anything in its path was either uprooted or destroyed. Fortunately, it seems to have missed any major towns. I don't suppose the true extent of the damage will be known for a few days. Certainly the electricity won't be on for a while. Did you sleep all right?'

'Yes, thank you.' Never one to pussy-foot around, she said bluntly, 'I haven't seen Helena.'

He looked away, and a muscle jumped in his jaw. 'No,' he agreed quietly. 'She isn't here.'

'Oh.'

Sounded like a sensitive subject, best avoided, perhaps, and she was disgusted with herself for the rush of hope she felt that they might have split up. Returning her attention to the garden, she observed lightly, 'The storm will have put your landscaping plans back.' When he didn't answer, she turned to look at him, curiosity in her dark eyes. 'No landscaping?'

'No.'

'Sorry, I didn't mean to pry.'

One hand on the back of the chair where he'd tossed his jacket, he said quietly, 'I tried to keep it separate.'

'Sorry?' she asked in confusion.

'The house and the conference centre. I tried to keep them separate.' His back to her, he walked across to the Aga and put the kettle back on to boil.

Thoroughly bewildered, she asked lamely, 'Why?'

'Because it was easier.' Turning to face her, he gave a grim smile. 'Helena is missing.'

'*Missing?*'

'Yes. She walked out one day and didn't come back.'

'Didn't come *back*?' she echoed in amazement. 'But why on earth didn't you tell me? No,' she corrected herself with a little grimace. 'Why should you? It wasn't any of my business, was it? And you wanted to keep the conference centre and your private concerns separate.' Which was why he'd never invited her to the house. Or maybe it wasn't. Maybe it was because something was between them that wasn't *allowed* to be between them.

'Yes.'

'She left without telling you she was going?' Just because it was none of her business, that didn't stop her being *curious*.

'Yes.'

'Because of the row?'

'No,' he denied simply.

'Because of a lover?'

'I don't know.'

'And no one knows where she is?'

'No.'

'How long…? I mean, when did she…?'

'Leave? Two months ago. She didn't take anything with her. Not her passport, her clothes, any money. Or her car.'

When he said nothing further, she persisted, 'And?' Because there had to be an 'and', didn't there?

'And the police dug up the garden.'

Flicking her eyes to the window, then back to him, a very hollow feeling inside, she whispered in shock, 'They think you—killed her?'

'Probably not, but her father insisted that she wouldn't have just walked out. And the police have to cover all possibilities, don't they?'

'That's what they said?'

'Yes.'

A frown in her eyes, she returned her attention to the garden. 'Why would her father think she wouldn't walk out?'

'He doesn't like me, and he didn't think I was good enough for her. He thinks me cruel.'

'No,' she denied without hesitation. Whatever else he might be, she would have staked her life on the fact that he wasn't a cruel man. And how on earth could she not have known that all this was going on? People gossiped, started rumours... 'Does everyone believe it?' she asked. 'That you killed her?'

'I don't know if they believe it or not, but mud sticks.'

'But there's no evidence—is there?'

'No.'

'But until she's found...'

'I'm under suspicion, yes.'

Genuinely concerned, she said, 'I'm so sorry, Beck.'

With a deep sigh, he finished making his coffee.

'I'll see if I can find you somewhere else to stay until the roads are open.'

'Why?'

'I just told you why.'

Watching him, she gave a disturbed smile. 'For my reputation, or yours?' she asked softly.

'Yours.'

'Oh, I think my reputation can stand it. More to the point, does anyone else have a wood-burning stove?'

His mouth smiled. His eyes didn't. 'No, but you can't stay here.'

End of discussion? He spoke so quietly, impassively, with no sign of the strain he must be under, and her staying here had nothing whatever to do with reputations.

'Afraid I might ravish you?' she asked huskily.

'No, Carenza, I'm not afraid you might ravish me.'

'I'd like to... Sorry,' she apologised hastily, her face pink. 'I sometimes have a very big mouth.'

'To go with being a big girl?'

'Yes.' Being tall and rather generously made was the bane of her life. She'd always yearned to be tiny. Like Helena. No, not like Helena. Sigh deeper, she continued her contemplation of the ruined garden. 'She was very beautiful,' she murmured, and she had been. She'd only seen her the once—and once had been enough, she thought with a twisted smile. And no greater contrast to herself could ever have existed. Helena had been small and slender, perfection personified. Shoulder-length blonde hair that waved in exactly the right places. Wide blue eyes, a perfect nose... She'd watched from the window of the conference centre as Helena had tucked her hand into Beck's arm, smiled at him. A woman sure of her own attraction. Sure of being loved. Carenza was statuesque, and her thick dark hair didn't wave at all.

'Is there anyone you need to let know where you are?' he asked quietly.

She shook her head.

'Just as well,' he said with slight wryness, 'because I have no way of contacting them for you. I don't have a mobile.'

'And I left mine on the hall table. I wasn't going to be gone long: drive down and collect my notebook, drive home.'

'Yes. The Aga doesn't have a back boiler, but there should be enough hot water left if you want a shower,' he continued. 'Bathroom's the first door at the top of the stairs.' Hesitating a moment, he added, 'Helena left all her clothes here, and although you might not want to wear her things there are whole drawers of new underwear, things she'd bought and never used. There's no easy way to offer this, but you're very welcome to take anything you need. It might take a while to find you somewhere else to stay. Her bedroom is next to the bathroom.'

'Thank you. Clean underwear would be nice.'

'Then help yourself. I'll get us some breakfast.'

Nodding, she walked out and into the hall, and then up the stairs. She felt ragged and weak. And the strain of being alone with him until however long it took for him to find her somewhere else to stay was going to be enormous. And yet she didn't want to be anywhere else.

Halting outside Helena's room, she hesitated. She'd have been lying if she'd said she wasn't curious about the other woman's bedroom. Not theirs, Helena's. Maybe they didn't sleep together, but in this day and age it was usual for engaged couples to do so, and Beck didn't look like a man who was celibate. He looked as though he would be a very competent and gentle lover. Innovative, perhaps... And she really rather despised herself for wanting a man who belonged to someone else. For wanting a man who could be *attracted* to another woman when he was involved with someone else.

Feeling like an intruder, she pushed open the door. White. Everything was white. Drapes, bedlinen, carpet, even the furniture was white. The only colour was an ornate, and probably very expensive, turquoise glass lamp. Taking a deep breath, she slowly opened one door of the fitted wardrobe—except it wasn't a wardrobe, it was a small, walk-in closet. Clothes hung neatly to either side, all covered in plastic. Evening clothes, day clothes, smart, casual. Shoe racks held all her footwear. All neatly paired. Handbags were tucked beside them. Her own wardrobe looked as if the army might have been holding manoeuvres in there. To actually find a pair of shoes involved taking everything out from the bottom of the wardrobe and then stuffing it all back in. Shoes she never wore, shoes that no longer fitted... Looking at all this, she was embarrassed, and vowed that never, ever would she let anyone else look in her wardrobe. Best clear it out in case *she* disappeared.

Don't tempt fate, Carenza.

Backing out, she closed the door. She would just borrow some underwear, she decided. Helena's clothes wouldn't have fitted her anyway. Opening each drawer in the tall cabinet that stood by the window, she stared at all the tiny frilly triangles that seemed to constitute Helena's underwear. Glancing down at her own ample proportions, she laughed. She might just get into a thong. Selecting one, she shut the drawer and escaped from all this glamour.

Removing her jacket, she hung it over the rail at the top of the stairs and walked into the bathroom, which was a great deal more than functional. White granite had been moulded to form the basin, flow smoothly into the bath, and then up to form the shower. A vision in white modernity, as though it had been carved from snow. An ice sculpture. Gold fittings, bottle-green tiles and floor. Almost a shame to use it, really.

A curved groove in the granite allowed the glass door for the shower to be slid easily into place, and

with a wry smile for all this sybaritic luxury she
stripped off. There was no sign of Helena's toiletries
on the glass shelves, so she used Beck's.

Had the relationship been in trouble? she wondered as she rubbed her hair as dry as she could and
then dressed. Had her disappearance come as a surprise? It wasn't something she felt she could ask
because she really didn't know him all that well.
Only knew that he had the ability to make her heart
beat faster, induce fantasies, even after she'd known
he was engaged. Her infatuation had been extraordinarily foolish considering the contrast between
herself and Helena. Beck obviously went for the
pocket Venus type... So why, then, was he attracted
to herself? As unlike Helena as it was possible to
be? Tall, with brown hair and eyes, legacy of a
Greek great-grandmother, busty, definitely hippy—
exotic, someone had once said, but she couldn't see
it. Never saw her own quicksilver smiles, or the
flashes of amusement in her dark eyes.

Tilting her head to one side, she wondered what
she was really like. A contrary sort of person, she
decided, one moment serene, the next a flurry of
energy and enthusiasm. She also tended to say what
she was thinking, which wasn't always wise. Neither
was it wise to stay in the house of a man you were
very strongly attracted to. A man you wanted to
touch. Constantly. And she'd lingered too long.

Quickly washing out her own underwear and
hanging it on the towel rail, she gave a wry smile.

Her underwear was *pretty* but definitely big. Big knickers, big bra, not something Beck would be used to.

With a little shake of her head for thoughts that really didn't matter, she walked out. The smell of frying reached her as she descended the stairs, and her stomach rumbled in anticipation.

He turned as she entered the kitchen, eyes sombre. 'Hungry?'

'Very.'

'Good. The tea's made, only needs pouring.'

Whilst she poured the tea into the two mugs, he dished up eggs, bacon, sausage, tomato and fried bread.

'Tuck in,' he ordered as he placed the meals on the table.

They ate mostly in silence, and when they'd finished both sat, staring down into their tea. She couldn't think of anything to say, nothing that might not have thorns on it, anyway.

'I'm not much good at small talk,' he eventually apologised quietly.

She smiled. 'Neither am I. Did I thank you for rescuing me?'

'No thanks were needed.'

She lapsed back into silence, and then asked quietly, 'Where's Spanner? I never see him around.'

'Spanner?' he echoed softly. 'He died.'

'I'm sorry. Shall you get another dog?'

'No.'

Because his life was still unsettled? Because he might have a murder charge hanging over his head? 'Why Spanner?' she asked curiously. 'It seems an odd name for a dog.'

'Because when I found him as a tiny, abandoned puppy he was trying to chew a nut off a piece of scrap metal.'

'Oh.'

'And you? Is business good?'

'So-so. I've just finished a large commission. Barn conversion. I opened a small shop in Croydon.' She grinned, then qualified, 'I'm renting out a small area in a wallpaper and fabric shop. I persuaded the owner that it would be good for his business. When people came in to buy decorating materials, he could steer them in my direction. Or, alternatively, if they came to see *me*, I could make my selections from his stock.'

'Sounds a good arrangement.'

'Mm, seems to be working OK. And your days of inactivity will soon be over,' she teased. 'A few more weeks and the conference centre will be finished. You'll be able to go to work.'

He gave a small, rather cynical smile. 'I already do go to work. The restaurant is doing very well.'

'*Restaurant?*'

'Yes. Why the look of surprise? Don't I look as though I could run a restaurant?'

'No. Yes. I don't know,' she denied lamely. 'Just

that… Well, I don't know,' she laughed. 'I assumed you were waiting to run the conference centre.'

'No, neither will I run it when it's finished. I shall put in a manager.'

'Oh,' she murmured inadequately. She didn't know him at all, did she? She'd made a lot of assumptions about him, about his lifestyle, day-dreamed a lot of exciting possibilities, but the simple fact remained that his life was none of her business. Nor ever could be whilst he was still engaged to Helena. Realising the silence had gone on too long, she murmured, 'And it's doing well, you say?'

'Oh, yes,' he agreed, his cynicism more marked. 'Ever since Helena disappeared, bookings have rocketed. Everyone wants to get a glimpse of the murderer.'

'Except you aren't.'

'No, but people believe what they want to believe. And it's very good for business. At the moment, to get a table, you would have to book three months in advance.'

'And you have no idea where she might be?'

He shook his head.

Still picking idly at the rim of her mug, and without looking at him, she blurted, 'Are you still engaged to her? I mean, were you, before she left?'

'Why do you want to know?'

'Oh, no reason, I just…was trying to think of a reason why she might want to disappear. I wasn't being nosy… Yes, I was,' she corrected honestly, because she wanted to know about the impossibly beautiful Helena, about their relationship. Wanted to know why he had seemed so sad in November. Wanted to make it right. And how women did tend to fool themselves, she thought wryly, into thinking they were the only ones who could comfort. 'You don't think she's dead?'

'No.'

'Why?'

'No concrete reason,' he said as he got to his feet and collected their plates. 'You will need to contact your insurance company.'

'Yes.'

'You were fully insured?'

She nodded.

'But you will need a car to conduct your business, won't you? Does the insurance cover for hire?'

'Don't know.'

He gave her a look of reproof. 'Well, if it doesn't, you can use the Land Rover,' he offered as he scraped the plates into the bin, rinsed them off and put them into the dishwasher, and then he halted, gave a wry smile, and took them out again. 'You get so used to the little luxuries of life,' he murmured. 'Like electricity.'

'Yes,' she agreed, because she hadn't considered it either.

'The perishables from the fridge I've put in the garage where it's colder. So, if you need milk when the current bottle's finished, that's where it is.'

She nodded and got up to dry the dishes he was washing. She felt almost stifled by his nearness, needed speech to cover the fact. 'Won't you need your car?'

He shook his head. 'I don't go out much.'

'Because of Helena?'

'No, by inclination. And if I do need transport I can use Helena's car.' When he'd finished washing up, he walked across to the Aga. Using an oven glove, he bent to open one of the doors. Lifting the lid on something, he peered inside, stirred it, then closed the door again. She smiled. He didn't look prissy, or silly, doing it, just like a very masculine man doing something he did rather a lot of.

'Even when I find you somewhere else to stay, you might not be able to go home for a few days,' he added quietly as he turned. 'The road isn't just blocked with one or two trees—whole stretches of the forest have come down. I don't even think it's a possibility that you would be able to walk into Horsham and hire a car. Or get the train. I have no idea if they're running. In the meantime, if you need some privacy, there's a spare room you can use.' Putting down the oven gloves, he indicated for her to follow him and then showed her into the room next to Helena's.

Now, this she liked, she decided. Navy blue walls and carpet, light plum-coloured paintwork that was picked up in the bedspread and curtains, and wooden furniture.

'You can see the restaurant from here,' he murmured as he walked across to the window.

You can also see the bed. Stop it, Carenza. She didn't want an affair with a man who was engaged to someone else, even if he wanted it, which she didn't think he did. She was quite sure that it was a reluctant attraction. And he was a man of strong will otherwise he wouldn't have been able to stand in a bedroom with her and stare from the window.

Joining him, because there didn't seem any other option, she felt the blood begin to pump in her veins as his arm brushed hers. 'What's your blood doing?' she asked without thinking, and cursed her unruly tongue.

'I'm sorry?'

'Nothing. Is that it?' she added hastily.

'Yes, the roof just beyond the trees.'

'Not far to travel.' Amazing how you could hold a conversation when your whole body was screaming. 'I assume you go there every day?'

'Every weekend; I only open Friday, Saturday and Sunday. And yes, I go there, because I do the cooking.'

'A man of many parts. I didn't know you were a chef.' And if she didn't get out of here right *now* she was going to touch him.

'Self-taught.' He sounded strained, and she jerked her head round to look at him. Found that he was watching her. His eyes had the grey luminescence of sunshine through cloud, she thought whimsically, and she wanted to reach out and trail her fingers along that determined jaw, touch her lips to his well-shaped mouth…

'Don't,' he reproved huskily.

'No.' Snatching her eyes away, she stared determinedly out of the window. Forcing her voice to neutrality, she murmured, 'I thought you were a marine archaeologist.' There didn't seem to be very much she could do about her pulse rate. This really was masochism.

'I am.'

'Lots of different hats. What else can you do?'

'Whatever you want. No,' he denied hurriedly. Hands curled into fists on the window sill, his voice sounded like metal strained through glass.

Fighting to maintain her own equilibrium, she leapt hastily into the breach left by his words. 'You must be a very good cook, if it's doing so well. People wouldn't keep coming just to see a possible murderer if the food was lousy. You wouldn't believe what I want.'

'I would.'

Oh, God. Staring blindly at the roof of the building just visible through the trees, she stated determinedly, 'Lucky the tornado didn't cut through here.'

'Tornado?'

'That was what it felt like. A roaring, shrieking dervish that, if it hadn't been for the tree anchoring me in place, might have taken me to—Oz. Beck?'

'No.' He responded fiercely to her unasked question and rapidly changed the subject. 'You mentioned a dragon?'

'What?'

'Last night, you said…'

'Oh.'

'You were right in its path?'

'Yes. I was terrified.' Explaining quickly all that had happened in a voice that was too fast and really rather breathless, she added, 'And my reactions were far too slow.'

'Your reactions saved your life,' he corrected.

'Yes,' she agreed. This was madness. 'Was anyone killed, do you know?'

He shook his head. 'I haven't heard any news, and Doug…'

'Doug?'

'Local police, and he wasn't telling, even if he knew. All I know with any certainty is that it cut a great swathe through the forest towards Handcross. I told him you were here.'

She nodded, gave a little shiver.

'Come on, you're probably still in shock. Why don't you go and sit by the fire?'

No, she wanted to deny, I'm not in shock. But then, he knew that, didn't he? Knew she was fighting her feelings for him. Feelings that hurt. Because they were futile. She knew that. She really did know that. Following him out, she grabbed her jacket off the banister. 'I think I'll go for a walk. Go and look at your restaurant. I can get my notebook from the conference centre at the same time.'

'I don't have an umbrella…'

'It doesn't matter. Rain won't hurt me.'

'It will make you very wet.' Walking across the kitchen, he opened a cupboard and removed a rain-coat. 'Use this.'

Reluctantly taking it, she asked hesitantly, 'Was it…?'

'Helena's, yes. She hardly ever wore it.'

With a meaningless smile, she put it on. The sleeves were too short, the back too narrow, but she supposed it would keep the worst of the wet off. Pulling up the hood, she walked out.

Feelings were the damnedest things, weren't they? Hit you without warning, scrambled you up… And she didn't want to be wearing Helena's rain-coat.

Automatically circumnavigating fallen branches, whole trees, she sighed. She felt exhausted. And don't, don't, she cautioned herself, read anything into the fact that they had separate bedrooms. Lots of couples slept apart for one reason or another; it didn't mean they weren't in love. Didn't mean he didn't miss her dreadfully.

'Not that way, miss…'

Turning with a start, she gave a lame smile to the young policeman behind her.

'Electricity cables are still down,' he explained.

Remembering the blue sparks of the night before, she nodded.

'Although the power has been turned off. And there are a lot of unstable trees. Where were you headed?'

'Nowhere,' she denied. 'Just having a look. My car's somewhere around. Grey hatchback,' she added helpfully. '*Was* a grey hatchback.' And stupidly, idiotically, her eyes filled with tears. 'Sorry,' she sniffed. 'Only just hit me, I suppose... Sorry,' she apologised again as she realised the unintended pun.

'The grey car with the tree across it?' he asked in astonishment.

'Yes.'

'My God!' he exclaimed. 'You were lucky to get out.'

'Yes, but not unaided. A Mr Beckford rescued me.' And the policeman's face changed. Because he was a suspected murderer? she wondered. She couldn't think of any other reason. Unless he didn't have a licence for his restaurant; or tax for his car. 'I'm staying with him,' she added defiantly, 'until the roads are clear.'

'You'll be Miss Dean, then.'

'Yes.'

'He asked me to see if I could find alternative accommodation for you. He's...'

'I know what he is,' she interrupted. 'And I know what you think he is. And you're wrong. I'd better get back. How long before the road is open? Do you know?'

'Won't be today... And I don't *think* he's anything,' he reproved, 'and he knows as well as I do that it isn't wise for a young lady to stay with a gentleman who—might be vulnerable.'

'Sorry,' she apologised for the third time. 'But I work for him...'

'And you're naturally protective,' he finished for her. 'All I'm saying is, be careful.'

'I will.'

Turning away, she was aware of him watching her, and felt despair wash through her. If she was going to leap to his defence every time someone said something even slightly suspect, it wouldn't be long before the whole area would know she was in love with him. No, not in love, she denied forcefully to herself. She didn't know him. You couldn't be in love with someone you didn't know. Could you? But she did know he hadn't killed his fiancée. Do you, Carenza? How very clairvoyant of you. Kicking irritably at a tree branch, she pulled the wide hood back in place and held it with both hands.

Coming out on to a small slip-road, she turned along it. Branches littered the surface, together with sundry other rubbish. A car hub-cap, a black plastic sack, a child's woollen glove, and a sieve, all blown there by a capricious wind, she supposed. A few yards further on was his restaurant. And this she liked. No fancy name or sign, just a long stone building that had been left as it was meant to be. A plaque by the main door said simply, 'The Barn.'

There was no menu board, nothing at all to say what it was. A no-frills establishment with excellent food? A small red car was parked to one side, with, thankfully, no damage.

Hands still holding her hood in place, she walked along the side and peered in one of the leaded windows. No fancy tablecloths, no fancy lamps, just good quality wooden tables and chairs. It was too dim inside to see very much else and so she walked round to the other side, and saw Beck. Hands shoved into his pockets, he was staring rather grimly at the wall to one side of the small terrace that presumably, in the summer, allowed diners to eat outside.

Moving quietly to join him, she too stared at the wall. 'Mur' had been sprayed in black paint. A discarded aerosol can lay below it.

He glanced at her, then returned his attention to the wall.

'Not very nice,' she commented quietly. 'There's only one word I can think of off hand that begins with ''mur''.'

'Yes.'

'And either they were interrupted or the storm frightened them off.'

'Yes.'

'You don't seem very surprised, or shocked.'

'No, it happens with rather boring frequency.'

Turning to look at her, he said almost sombrely, 'You look like a very wet pixie.'

'Troll,' she corrected. 'I'm too big for a pixie.' Turning abruptly away, she said over her shoulder, 'I'll go and get my notebook.'

She was aware of him following her as she walked in the general direction of the conference centre. There was a separate road she used when she came, and so she'd never been in this part of the grounds before.

'This way,' he indicated quietly, and she turned and followed him along a small track that eventually came out on the road. A hundred yards further on was the conference centre. It had once been a dower house on what had been a large estate, and she was now helping to convert it to hold conferences.

He unlocked the front door before she could get out her own keys, and led the way inside.

On her own ground, so to speak, she looked quickly round with a critical eye, then nodded in satisfaction. The plasterers had finished the walls, as they'd promised.

Throwing open the door on the left, she walked inside to retrieve her notebook.

'Is there anything you need to check?'

'Upstairs bathroom, and one of the bedrooms in the new extension. I like your restaurant,' she murmured as she headed for the staircase. 'Were you open last night?'

'No, lunch only on Sundays.'

'Someone left their car behind.'

He nodded. 'One of the waitresses. It wouldn't start and so I ran her home. That's why I was out. What did the law want?'

'Oh, just some stupid policeman being officious,' she muttered as she began climbing. 'The kitchen equipment is being delivered next week.'

'Yes. What did he do? Warn you off?'

'No.'

'Liar.'

With a disturbed smile, she sighed. 'Not really; he just said it might not be wise for me to stay here. That you might be—vulnerable.'

'Ah.'

Are you? she wanted to ask him. But didn't. She did halt to look back at him, and this time he didn't look away, just held her gaze for long, long moments. She wanted to smile at him, but smiling could be dangerous. Wrenching her eyes away, she trod carefully across the littered landing. He was watching her, she knew he was, but she dared not look back again.

'What will happen if they don't ever find her?'

'I don't know. I don't allow myself to think too far ahead.'

No, well, you wouldn't, would you?

'I only hope that your reputation doesn't suffer because of me.'

'Is that why you stay away from me when I'm here?' she asked as she pushed open the bedroom door. 'Because of my reputation?' And knew it wasn't true. 'I know you didn't kill her,' she stated confidently as she walked across the bedroom and into the bathroom.

'No, you don't,' he reproved as he followed her. 'How many times have you read in the papers that neighbours of murderers had thought them the nicest, quietest of people?'

'That's different.'

'No, it isn't.'

'But you didn't kill her!' she persisted.

'No,' he agreed. 'I didn't. But on the off chance that I did people here will keep their distance, just in case, by association, they get mixed up in this mess.'

'They don't keep their distance from your restaurant,' she pointed out as she stared with a critical eye at the fittings. 'You said it did very well.'

'It does, but that's voyeuristic, dicing with danger—I don't know, but if those same customers saw me in the street they would cross over, ignore me.'

'Well, I don't intend to ignore you! And if you ever need a character witness...' Turning, she waited for him to move so that she could return to the landing. Tension rippled between them. Tension and something else. But he still didn't move.

'And what could you say?' he asked pointedly. 'That you've worked for me for a few weeks? But that we very rarely meet? And what did you learn about him? the lawyer would ask. Oh, not much—

that he seemed very fond of his dog, liked walking in the rain…'

'Do you?'

'Carrie! What do you really know about me?'

'That you have the ability to make me ache,' she whispered. 'Fantasise. And that although we don't very often meet I watch for you. Hope, like an adolescent, to catch a glimpse of you walking in the grounds. That I'm violently attracted to you and that if I stay standing close to you for much longer I'm going to do something really stupid. Like kiss you.'

He moved quickly to one side, and she escaped. Hurrying, despairing, not looking where she was going, she trod on a piece of wood that had been left lying on the floor, lurched, and he caught her, held her safe.

'Thanks,' she muttered.

When he didn't release her, she turned her head to look up into his rather bleak face—and couldn't look away. The first time they'd met, the look they'd shared had been one of warmth, possible friendship, and that little leap of attraction that was so exciting, so—hopeful. The look they exchanged now was one of wariness, want and an aching despair that it wasn't going to happen. That *nothing* was going to happen. Because of Helena.

'It won't work,' he said quietly.

'I know.'

'I have to find her, Carenza.'

'Yes.' Both were tense, both holding back, and then he opened his hands and released her.

'Come on, back to the house—if I can give you nothing else,' he added almost inaudibly, 'I can at least offer you a warm fire.'

The least? she wondered bleakly. Or all?

CHAPTER THREE

LOOKING away, she said neutrally, 'I just need to check something in one of the bedrooms in the extension. I'll join you outside.' Walking quickly away, she ran down the staircase, pushed open the door to the annexe that ran at right angles to the main building, and cursed herself for a fool. Hands clenched, she strode blindly along the narrow, glassed-in passageway to the room at the end.

She should never have agreed to work for him. Not after she'd known about Helena. Was honour more important than happiness? she wondered. Helena had left him, and that surely broke the engagement, didn't it? Unless she'd been kidnapped, or worse... But how could he be attracted to herself if he loved Helena? Some men did. Some men were incapable of fidelity. But not Beck.

You don't know him, Carenza. Don't know what sort of man he is. And hearts weren't the most reliable organs for judgement. 'What else can you do?' she'd asked. 'Whatever you want...' Face troubled, she checked the light fitting, and quietly closed the door behind her. Hands shoved into her pockets—Helena's pockets—she stared out at the small courtyard beyond the windows. The paving had almost been finished. With tubs of flowers, tables and chairs, it would make a nice place for the delegates to sit.

She wanted to touch him, climb all over him, and she had never felt like that in her life before. Every time she saw him, it got worse.

Depressed, aching, she turned away and joined Beck outside. Tension shivered between them as they walked back in silence. The rain still fell heavy and straight, pattering monotonously on the ground. A dreary match for her feelings.

A man was waiting for them as they emerged from the treeline at the back of the house, a carrier bag clasped in his arms. Of a similar age to Beck, in his mid-thirties, maybe, his fair hair was plastered wetly to his scalp, much as Beck's was, rain dripping down his rather puckish face. He looked curiously at Carenza, and grinned.

'An orphan of the storm?'

'Something like that.' Making an effort, she forced a smile. 'My car was struck by a tree.' There was a great deal of speculation in his glance and she knew he was wondering if she'd been here *before* the storm struck, or after.

'After,' she said softly, and he flushed.

'The door was open,' Beck put in quietly. 'You didn't need to hover on the step getting soaked.' Pushing open the door, he introduced casually, 'This is Carenza, the interior designer who's doing the conference centre. Carenza, meet John, my neighbour.'

'Who is desperately hoping you haven't let the Aga go out. We only have electricity—had,' he corrected softly to Carrie. 'And trying to cook a meal for the kiddies over a candle is a joke.'

Beck smiled, a smile that looked as forced as hers had felt, opened the door of the oven, and, reaching for the oven gloves, extracted a blue casserole dish. Removing the lid, he showed John the contents. 'I was just going to bring it over for you.'

The other man looked startled. 'Hey,' he murmured in embarrassment, 'you didn't need to do that.'

'You don't want it?'

'Yes! Of course I want it, you fool! So long as you aren't charging me your fancy prices. Do you know how much it *costs* to eat in his restaurant?' he asked Carrie.

She shook her head, knew it was only awkwardness talking. An awkwardness he'd picked up from themselves. Even a fool couldn't have missed the tension between them.

'A *fortune*! And that's without the wine!'

Beck merely smiled. 'What are you clutching so zealously to your chest?' he asked mildly.

'Well, it isn't Hele—' Breaking off, he looked mortified. 'God, I'm sorry. I didn't mean... Me and my big mouth,' he muttered. Taking a deep breath, he added, 'I brought your flasks back. Thank you for that.' Voice subdued, he opened the bag and peered inside as though the contents might have changed without him noticing. 'And some potatoes and eggs. I thought I might borrow the Aga...' Raising his eyes, face pink, he pleaded, 'Beck, I'm sorry.'

Beck smiled, shook his head. Reaching into the bag, he removed the two flasks and put them on the work surface. Walking across to the cupboard that had held Helena's raincoat, he removed a small cardboard box. Placing the casserole inside, and then gently removing the carrier bag from John's arms, he put everything in the box and handed it to his neighbour. 'Go feed your family,' he said gently.

He nodded, gave Carenza a small smile, and left.

'He's a good friend,' Beck said simply. Taking off his jacket, he hung it back over the chair and held out his hand for the raincoat. 'His wife, Lisa, works for me in the restaurant—takes the bookings, does some waitressing.'

'And the flasks?' she asked curiously.

'I took over some tea and hot milk for them this morning. Peter doesn't like cold milk on his corn-flakes.'

And why did he find that so embarrassing? she wondered. Because he'd been caught doing a kind act? 'Peter's his son?'

'Mm,' he agreed as he hung up the raincoat. 'They also have a daughter named Jessica. Twins. Three years old.'

'Nice.'

'Yes. Hungry?'

'So-so.'

'I'll make us a sandwich. Why don't you go and sit by the fire? There are books, magazines…'

Because he wanted her out of the way? Because he was finding it desperately hard to cope with her presence? The way she was finding it desperately hard to cope with his?

She wandered into the lounge, and then wandered out again. Quietly pulling out a chair, she sat to watch him.

Without comment, he put the kettle on to boil and she saw that a very large saucepan now rested beside it. There was the wonderful aroma of stew.

'The meat from the restaurant freezer,' he explained. 'If it isn't cooked, it will go off.' Turning away from her, he began assembling the things he would need for their lunch. His movements were sure, economical and she wanted to touch him, run her hand down his arm, smile at him. Wanted to *know* him. Wanted to ask about Helena, but didn't think she wanted the answers.

To a casual observer, he would appear very calm, very contained, for a man under threat. But she wasn't a casual observer, and she knew it was a lie. 'Where did he sleep?' she asked curiously.

He turned, gave her a puzzled look.

'Spanner,' she murmured. 'Sorry, bad habit; I

tend to blurt out things I've been thinking without anyone knowing what subject I've now arrived at.'

He smiled. 'He slept in here.' He then added something that sounded like 'That was one thing I *wouldn't* be moved on', but she wasn't sure. Taking some cold beef from the fridge, he slanted her a query. 'Not vegetarian, are you?'

She shook her head, watched as he took a wicked-looking knife from the rack and began to slice it.

'Mustard? Pickle?'

'No, thanks. Just as it comes.'

When they'd eaten and drunk the tea, needing focus, occupation, to take her mind off Beck, she flipped open her pad and stared at the drawing on the first page. 'Carpets can go down next week.'

Reaching for the pad, he turned it and stared down at her sketch of how the centre would eventually look, and she stared hungrily at his face. 'You've made a few changes.'

'Yes, nothing drastic—different drapes. I thought these would frame the windows better.' Getting to her feet, she went to stand behind him. She almost rested her hand on his shoulder, then thought better of it. Touching was definitely out. 'They aren't set in stone. I can change them if you don't like them.'

'No, they're fine.'

Taking a deep breath to calm herself, forcing herself to concentrate on something other than Beck, she added, 'I also asked the electrician to put more sockets in the conference room itself.'

'Good idea.'

Voice slightly strained, she asked, 'Still happy with the colour?'

'Yes, green's restful. And as you said when we started the project we don't want anything too drastic, nothing that intrudes…'

As he was intruding. Dear God, but it was getting worse. She wanted to touch the hair at the back of his neck, still damp from the rain. He had nice ears…

He lurched to his feet, nearly knocking her over. 'I have to go out,' he said abruptly. 'Paperwork. Will you be all right?'

'Yes,' she agreed thickly.

'Give the stew a stir every now and again, will you?'

'Yes.'

Picking up his jacket, he walked out, but he didn't take the tension with him. Feeling stifled and shaky, she sat in his chair, stared blankly at the sketch before her, traced her finger where he had traced his.

He wanted her. She affected him as he affected her. It wasn't a heady feeling. And it couldn't go on.

Was he hating himself for how she could make him feel? If he still loved Helena…

And she did make him feel. She knew that as well as if he'd written it on the pad in front of her. She wasn't a conceited girl, but men did seem to find her—alluring. *Alluring?* Dear God, where had that word come from?

With a determined effort, she took the pencil that was clipped to the top of the pad and began to craft in more detail, but her mind wasn't really on what she was doing. Tossing her pencil aside in disgust, she dragged her hands through her hair. Her work always, *always* absorbed her. Whole hours could go by without her noticing, but, now, all she could think about was Beck.

Forcing herself to her feet, she went to stir the stew. What to do? It wasn't going to go away, was it? And she'd never felt like this in her life. Confused, and urgent, and wanting. She could almost taste him. *Wanted* to taste him.

Did he have a high sex drive? Was that why? Any woman would have had the same effect? No, she didn't believe that. Conceit?

And what if Helena was never found? What then? What if she was? Perhaps he'd strangled her in a fit of passion, lost his temper... No. But why would she have left?

Mindlessly stirring the stew that no longer needed stirring, she jumped nearly a foot in the air when the back door suddenly opened.

'Sorry,' John apologised.

Hand to her heart, she said, 'You nearly frightened me to death.'

'I brought back the casserole dish.'

'So I see.' Fighting for control, she forced a smile. 'Beck's over at the restaurant, I think. Paperwork,' she explained.

'Oh.'

'How was lunch?'

'Terrific,' he grinned. 'He's a brilliant cook... Although I expect you know that.'

'No, I've only sampled his breakfasts.' Suddenly realising how that must have sounded, she gave a lame smile. 'This morning, I meant—we haven't, didn't...'

Almost breaking in on her words, he blurted, 'You don't have to explain... I know he wouldn't... I mean, he loves her!' he exclaimed helplessly. 'It's just that he's a friend, someone I like very much, and I don't want to see him hurt even more. And that sounds as though I think you *will* hurt him,' he added disgustedly. 'Shall I come in again?'

She smiled, shook her head. 'How long have you know him?'

'Since we were kids. Did you know her?' he blurted.

'Helena? No.'

'She was beautiful... *Is* beautiful,' he hastily corrected. 'He must feel so wretched.'

'Yes.'

'Everyone loved her.' With an odd grimace, he shoved his hands into his jacket pockets as though he didn't know what else to do with them, and she wondered if John hadn't also fallen in love with her. Some women had the power for that.

Staring through the rain-lashed window, he muttered, 'I couldn't help noticing, earlier, that you seemed a bit...'

'Tense, yes. We'd been arguing about some detail at the centre,' she fabricated because some instinct made her wary of revealing anything else. 'We're just—colleagues.'

'Yes, of course. Sorry, it's none of my business, just that where Beck's concerned I get a bit paranoid. Even dug up his lawn, poor bastard.'

'Yes, he said.'

Without looking at her, he continued, 'He didn't kill her, you know.'

'No.'

'And if you know that, and I know that, why is everyone else so ready to believe the worst?'

'I don't know.'

His grievances not at an end, he continued, 'And why believe her father over Beck? Her father didn't know her. Fathers don't, not when their daughters have left home. People change.'

'Yes,' she agreed inadequately.

'Just because the stupid idiot thought Beck wasn't good enough for her... She couldn't have *had* a better man than Beck. Said she'd accused him of being cruel. *Cruel?* I ask you. He's the most unlikely candidate for cruelty you could ever meet. She'd never have said that. He adores her. Gave up travelling so that he could be with her all the time. Sold his house…'

'Sorry?'

'His house. In the Lake District. It was too isolated.'

'And this *isn't*?' she asked in disbelief.

'Nah, not compared to there. This was his parents' place. And if I ever catch the little sod who keeps writing on his walls…'

Perhaps realising that he was talking too much, saying things he shouldn't say to a virtual stranger, he hunched his neck into his shoulders in a sort of frustrated irritation. 'He won't even *defend* himself,' he muttered aggrievedly. He sighed again. 'It's as though he isn't even here. Quiet, polite… He was *never* like that. He could be a contentious so-and-so,' he smiled, then sighed.

'And what else?' she asked curiously. 'He couldn't have been contentious all the time.'

'No, of course not. He was tough—not bully-boy tough, nothing like that. A quiet strength, you know? Rock-solid. Determined, kind, brave. I've seen him risk his life to save others. He's one of those people you don't meet very often. Total integrity. Honest and uncompromising. The sort of person you yearn for in a crisis—and who doesn't run off at the mouth like I do. I'd better go,' he mumbled. 'I told Lisa I wouldn't be long.'

'Would you like me to fill the flask up again for you?'

'Would you? Thanks, that would be great.'

Whilst she put the kettle on and readied the flask, gave the stew another stir, he sat at the kitchen table and idly rifled through her pad. 'These for the conference centre?'

'Mm.'

'Nice.'

'Thank you,' she said drily, and he grinned.

'Me, I can't draw a straight line. And if it hadn't been for Beck…'

She waited, wondered why he felt the need to talk.

'He gave me a job when no one else would employ me. I was a drunk.' Just a simple statement. It wasn't said with defiance, or shame, just simply. A fact of life. 'Lisa was threatening to leave me, and who could blame her? Self-pity,' he muttered. 'It's a killer. So is living in a bottle. We lost the house. Nice little place up on the Downs… Beck heard about it, came to see me, said if I gave up drinking he would give me a job, let us live in the gatehouse. We would have to do it up, and then I'd be responsible for the grounds, help out where I was needed, until I could find something better. Which I now have. I repair farm machinery. It's what I'm good at. I've been in Canada the last few weeks…'

'They don't have their own mechanics?' she asked with a smile.

'Yes, but this is a new harvester. I went out to

help set it up, sort out teething troubles. That's why we haven't met.'

'No reason why we should,' she said quietly. 'As I said, I'm only workforce. If it hadn't been for the storm…'

'Yes, I know. And she'll come back. I know she will.'

'And then everything will be all right?' she put in quietly.

'Yes.'

Which meant that Carrie was probably being the biggest fool of all time. After filling the flask, she screwed on the top and handed it to him.

Taking it, he said quietly, 'I owe him so *much*! I'd do anything for him, you know. For them both.'

'Yes, I expect you would.'

Levering himself to his feet, he tucked the flask in his pocket and zipped up his wet jacket.

Face thoughtful, she watched him skirt the dug-up lawn. She'd just been warned off, hadn't she? Not that she'd needed it of course. She'd been warning herself off ever since she'd met him.

Catching movement from the corner of her eye, she watched Beck approach. He had a large box in his arms, and a rather preoccupied look on his face, but he walked with the easy confidence of a man sure of his own strengths, and weaknesses. And just why had he given up his marine archaeology? she wondered. Because his fiancée didn't like his travelling? Or travelling with him? Or because he couldn't bear to be parted from her? Was John right? Had he adored Helena? Did he still? In which case, why was he attracted to herself? And John had made Beck sound boring, self-righteous, perfect, and he wasn't like that at all.

He didn't look at her as he came in, merely placed the box on the surface and shrugged out of his jacket. 'Was that John leaving?'

'Yes, he brought your dish back.' She couldn't take her eyes off him.

He nodded without glancing her way, and tossed his jacket over the chair.

'He said you adored her.'

He didn't comment, merely walked over to put the kettle back on the hob, check his stew.

'What's Lisa like?'

'Nice. What else did he tell you?'

'Oh, nothing much,' she denied evasively.

'Carenza,' he reproved almost gently, 'you don't have the face for dissimulation. He makes no secret of the fact that he adored Helena. That he thinks he owes me something...'

'And that you stopped travelling.'

'Yes,' he agreed quietly. 'That I stopped travelling.'

'Why?'

'It's a long story,' he evaded. 'Coffee?'

'Please.' At least he hadn't told her that it was because of adoration for Helena.

He rinsed out the mugs they'd used earlier and

set them ready, then walked to the cupboard where he'd hung his fiancée's raincoat and collected some candles. 'It will be dark soon,' he murmured as he handed them to her. 'Find some pots or saucers to put them in, will you?'

Taking them, she laid them on the table and went to do as he asked. She found several small spice dishes and even one candle holder and set them round the kitchen. Beck found her some matches and she carefully lit them.

'What would you like for dinner?'

'What are you offering? Stew? Or stew?'

He gave a strained smile. 'That, or chicken stir fry.'

'Chicken, please.'

Sitting at the table, she watched him wash his hands then unwrap the fowl that had been sitting on top of the box and begin to joint it with a small, evidently sharp cleaver. You could kill someone with that. Abandoning the thought only half completed, she sighed. The candlelight should have been comforting. It wasn't.

'You should get out of those wet jeans,' she murmured. God, she sounded like her mother.

'They'll be all right.'

Yes, she supposed they would. From his point of view. Not from hers. They clung rather lovingly to his thighs. 'Did *you* adore her?' she had to ask.

He halted what he was doing for a moment, and then he sighed. 'Leave it, Carenza, please.' There had been no inflexion in his voice. Intent on his task, he neither looked round nor altered his stance in any way. There seemed no tension in his back, no awkwardness in his movements. And when the kettle boiled he made the coffee, carried hers over to the table and continued with his task.

Before she could think of anything else to ask, there was a knock at the door. Laying down his knife, he went to answer it.

It was the young policeman. He looked awkward. 'Hello, Beck. Sorry to trouble you…'

'Why don't you come in?' he invited. He looked almost grateful for the interruption.

Removing his cap, looking even more embarrassed, he stepped inside. His radio mike was squawking and crackling as though there were demons inside. He glanced at the flickering candles, offered a small smile to Carenza, then blurted awkwardly, 'Word spread, and, well, now there seem to be thirty of us.'

'Oh,' Beck commented blandly.

'People talk, you see, and before you know it…'

'You have thirty.'

'Yes.' Staring at his dripping cap, and then the floor where the drips were puddling, he mumbled, 'I can't tell them not to come, because I don't know who they all are. Someone…'

'Told someone, who told someone else,' Beck put in humorously.

'Yes,' the constable agreed thankfully. 'Seems

that everyone within walking distance wants to come. Although it will be damned dangerous with so many trees unstable.'

'But worth it,' Beck pointed out, 'so that they can say they ate with a murderer.'

'No!' he denied automatically, and then sighed. 'Yes,' he agreed. 'Probably. You can't expect people not to be curious about you…'

'And to want to sample the meals that would normally cost them a great deal of money.'

'And then they can say—' Breaking off, his face flushing, he gave a sheepish smile when Beck laughed.

'Human nature, and it isn't a problem. You look as though you could use a coffee.' Returning to the Aga, he put the kettle back to boil. 'How's the clear-up going?'

'Slowly. The trouble is, you're low priority here. Motorways and major roads have to be cleared first, and then they'll slowly work their way in. It's a hell of a mess out there. They don't even know when the phones and electricity will be back on. Not too much of a problem for you, of course.'

'No. Sugar? Milk?'

'Both, thanks.'

After making the coffee, he handed it to the constable, rewashed his hands, and returned to jointing his chicken.

Staring from one to the other, Carrie commented quietly, 'You didn't tell me you were going to feed everyone. Sorry,' she added sheepishly, 'none of my business. I didn't mean to sound like your wife.'

'You didn't,' Beck said quietly into the awkward silence that fell.

No, she thought tiredly. She didn't look like her either.

'The meat from the restaurant would only go off if it wasn't cooked, and so I thought I might as well feed all those who were unable to cook for themselves.'

'And the number has gone up to thirty.'

'Yes.'

'Is there anything I can do to help?'

'Not just at the moment.' Returning to his jointing, he finished it, then bent to take some vegetables from the bottom of the open fridge. Collecting a chopping board, he began to shred them.

The constable finished his coffee in silence. 'Thank you,' he said awkwardly. 'I haven't been able to find anywhere else for Miss Dean to stay. I'll keep trying.'

'Thanks.'

'You could always ask those that turn up tonight.'

'Yes, I'll do that. Thanks for trying.'

'My pleasure. I'll see you later.'

'Any time after seven.'

The door closed quietly behind him.

Silence, but for the tap-tapping of Beck's knife, and then she realised something she should have realised earlier.

'How did he get in?'

'Sorry?'

'The policeman. I've just realised, if he can get in…'

'Oh, no. That's Doug. I told you, he's a local. He can't get *out*. Well, not without a very long walk, anyway. He gets information, instruction, over his radio.'

'Oh.' Silence again. 'Should I get out soup bowls or plates, or something?' she asked eventually.

Nodding toward the box he'd brought in, he said, 'In there.'

Getting up, she went to empty it. There were five French sticks still in their Cellophane wrappers, which had obviously been frozen, a large gateau in a plastic container, cream, cutlery and crockery. Taking everything out, she laid it on the work surface.

'There are only twenty-five soup dishes,' she said in a subdued voice.

'There are some more in the dresser. Cutlery in one of the drawers.'

'Will we need small plates for the gateau?'

'Yes.' He suddenly halted what he was doing and turned to face her. 'Stop sounding like a frightened child. Snap back, Carrie; don't take what I dish out as though…'

'I care?' she completed for him. 'But I do care, and I wasn't frightened of you, just mortified that I should say something so stupid. Especially with a policeman standing there.'

'And if everyone stopped to think before they spoke there would be no conversation,' he pointed out. 'Let me fight my own demons, Carrie. Don't try to fight them for me.'

'And if she isn't dead,' she said under her breath, 'I think I will kill her.'

'Sorry?'

'Nothing. I was just wondering how they had the gall to come when they think so badly of you.'

'They feel awkward. Nothing could *be* more awkward, could it? Belay that, if the Gods are listening, *something* will come along to top it. And stop walking on eggshells. It doesn't make it easier.'

Make what easier? she wanted to ask. But didn't, because maybe, just maybe, she wouldn't like the answer. John's talk of adoration had rather dented her confidence. 'I'll put out thirty plates, then, shall I?'

'Please.' Taking a large wok from a lower cupboard, he put it on the Aga and dribbled in some olive oil. 'And at six-thirty you can cut up the bread and put it in a bowl.'

She threw him a salute and began laying out dishes. 'John said this place belonged to your parents.'

'Yes, they moved here three years ago. My father left it to me when he died. If you move the chairs and push the table to one side, it will give us more room.'

She nodded, went to do as he'd suggested. 'Did you open the restaurant because you needed something to do after you stopped travelling?' she probed.

'Yes. The restaurant was already here. Just needed refurbishing. It hadn't been used in a while. My father had been going to do it. One of his projects, but…' Glancing at the clock, he began to transfer the chicken pieces to the wok, and after that he steered the conversation into less personal channels until the first of their 'guests' arrived.

There was awkwardness at first, muted talk, and then, as more and more people arrived, the atmosphere became more friendly. Someone had even brought a bottle of wine.

As Beck filled each bowl, Carrie handed them out, and then sat to eat her own. And watched them. Watched how they watched Beck if they thought he wasn't looking, and it wasn't true, what he'd said, she thought. Not about the women anyway. They didn't only come because of the mysterious disappearance of his fiancée, because they found him intriguing, or because they thought he had hidden depths, which, of course, he did. Most people had depths that weren't obvious. No, they came because he was a devastatingly attractive man with an intriguing air of danger about him. He excited them. As he excited her.

Glancing at him, she tried to see him as they saw him. A tall man, with an easy grace. A man who had done a great many things in his life. A man who didn't talk about himself. And that made him intriguing. Contentious, John had said. She wanted to see him like that.

'You're looking very pensive,' a tall, elderly woman commented from beside her.

With a little start, so lost in her own thoughts she had almost forgotten about the other people, she gave a small smile. 'I was trying to define him to myself. Trying to put a name to what makes him so—different.'

'His air of invincibility,' the old lady pronounced without hesitation. 'As though nothing will ever defeat him.'

'Yes,' Carrie agreed thoughtfully. There was no severity in his face, but you knew without knowing how you knew that he was a very determined man. Adversity would only make him stronger. 'Sorry,' she apologised with one of her quick smiles, 'I'm Carenza. I'm doing the interior design of the conference centre.'

'And staying here?' she asked archly.

'Until the roads are clear, yes.'

She smiled. 'No offence meant. I only came to be nosy. I expected to find him loathsome,' she commented, her eyes on Beck. 'Men who have done all that he seems to have done in his life often are.'

'You haven't met before?'

'No. Read about him in the local rag, heard about him—who hasn't? And I find it extraordinarily bizarre that he also invited one of the policemen who accused him. I wouldn't. Name's Beatie, by the way. And that's my daughter,' she added with an abrupt nod towards the group by the door. 'The one with the dyed blonde hair and stuck-up nose.'

Carrie choked on a piece of chicken. 'You sound as though you don't like her.'

'I don't. She's furious that I insisted on coming. Cramps her style.' She snorted. 'What style? She doesn't have any. You do.'

With a small smile, Carrie said gravely, 'Thank you.'

'No need for thanks—me, I speak as I find. You look a bit mysterious, always an advantage. Like him, do you?'

'Yes,' she agreed cautiously.

She nodded. 'Best to be honest, isn't it? Like me. I came out of curiosity, and to sample his cooking. Not many of us can afford his fancy prices. Not that I blame him; I'd do the same if the opportunity ever arose—and if I could cook!' Scraping her bowl clean, she put it on the table. 'I don't suppose he's making any coffee, is he?' she asked rather wistfully.

Carrie smiled and got to her feet. 'I'll ask.'

Squeezing between the people, she touched Beck on the arm, felt her stomach clench at the feel of him.

'Beatie wants to know if there's any coffee.'

'And who's Beatie?'

She indicted the elderly lady. 'She thinks you look invincible.'

'Then let's hope she's right.' Reaching for the kettle, he moved his way through the throng and filled it. Returning, he put it on to boil. There were only twelve cups because he hadn't brought any over from the restaurant, and so they took it in turns.

Half an hour later they'd all gone, with only the dirty dishes to show they'd ever been there. They hadn't gone willingly, she thought with a small smile. And Beck's orchestration of their departure had been masterly.

'Why are you smiling?' he asked her.

'At the expert way you dismissed them. Me, I'd have probably ended up being rude.'

'I merely told them it was time they went home.'

'Mm,' she agreed. 'Like lambs to the pen. You expect to be obeyed, don't you?'

'Do I?'

'Yes,' she said positively. 'And you were right about me not staying here.'

He stilled.

'I'm finding it very hard to stifle my feelings.'

'Try,' he said roughly as he re-filled the kettle.

She had been trying, and it wasn't working. 'Did you ask anyone if they had room for me?'

'No.'

No. And soon it would be night. 'Did you see her go?'

'Helena? No.'

'You came back from somewhere and she was gone?'

'Yes, and this isn't a conversation we should be having,' he reproved quietly. His voice was still a little bit rough, slightly husky.

In her opinion, it was the *only* conversation they should be having.

He piled all the dishes in the sink, squirted in washing-up liquid, and then poured the boiling contents of the kettle over them. Adding cold water, he began to wash up.

Silently joining him, she began to dry. 'I've never felt like this before.'

'Please don't. I'm not free, Carrie.'

'She left you…' Abandoning it, she concentrated on the plate she was drying. She felt enclosed in a void, held still, waiting. The flickering candles, the shadows, barely intruded. Hell might have looked like this. She could see their reflections in the window, side by side—and a hundred miles apart. 'I feel as though I'm being sawn in half with a rusty knife,' she whispered. 'And I want to kiss you. Do you have *any* idea how much I want to kiss you? It's all I can think about. You have such a beautiful mouth…' Unable to breathe, she tossed down the tea towel. 'I'm going out.'

'Don't be absurd,' he argued raggedly. 'It's pitch-black out there; you could break your neck! You think I need another woman disappearing?'

Unable to keep still, arms wrapped round herself, she began stalking up and down the kitchen. She felt claustrophobic and restless. Aching and hurting. 'Do you know what I hate?' she suddenly asked. 'People being reasonable.' Up and down, round and round, shoving chairs back under the table, her boot heels making harsh, echoing thuds. 'And people who spell enquiry with an i.'

'What?' he demanded in bewilderment.

'It really bugs me. It's spelt with an *e*. It was always spelt that way! So how come it's now spelt with an i? Hmm?'

'You aren't making sense.'

'Of course I'm not making sense!' she shouted. Rushing out, she ran up the stairs and into her room and slammed the door.

Still pacing, still agitated, she roamed round the small room. Perhaps if she kissed him it would all go away. She might not even like the feel of his mouth on hers... Might be the biggest turn-off of all time... Wrenching open the door, she hurried back down and slammed into the kitchen. He was still at the sink, hands in the soapy water, and there was an expression of such anguish on his face that she halted.

'I *need* you,' she cried. 'All my life I've waited for someone like you!'

He closed his eyes.

'It can't be wrong! She isn't *here*! How can it be wrong, Beck?' Moving towards him, body shaking, she touched her hands to his rigid shoulder. Suds sprinkled his forearms, clung to the fine hairs, and without thinking she reached out, gently spread the suds up towards the inside of his elbow with her fingers. It felt utterly erotic.

He watched what she was doing, unmoving, and then he turned his head towards her. He was so close, her mouth a bare inch from his, and his eyes looked as if they were smouldering in the flickering light. She parted her lips as though unable to help it, and so he kissed her. And restraint shattered.

CHAPTER FOUR

SHE clutched at his sweater and closed her eyes. It was a kiss that robbed her of sense, took away everything that had ever mattered in her life. Wet hands held out at his sides, every other part of him touched her. Her mind, her body, her senses. It was harsh, and urgent, and utterly devouring. His mouth did things to her that no man's had ever done. It was complete and crucifying.

He finally put his arms around her and she felt the wetness of his hands against her back. Felt the firmness of his thighs, his swift arousal, and pressed closer, ever closer. Standing on her toes, she wound both arms round his neck, touched her fingers to his nape, and shivered with the rightness of it all.

Avidly nibbling at his lips, his cheek, she whispered raggedly, 'It feels like coming home.'

And he stilled, reaching up to grasp her arms and move them away. Still holding her wrists, he searched her eyes, her face, let his breath out on a long, long sigh. 'I can't do this,' he said raggedly.

'Why?'

'Because until I find her... Try to understand, Carrie. I feel responsible.'

'How can I understand when you won't tell me

72

anything?' Eyes fixed desperately on his face, she pleaded, 'Talk to me. Tell me all that happened.'

'I can't. Not until I've spoken to her.'

'If she's alive.'

'If she's alive,' he agreed.

'But you think she is?'

'Yes.'

'Why? Why not a kidnapping? Amnesia?' Wrenching her hands free, she gave him a shake. 'Talk to me, Beck!'

'I can't.'

Frustrated, angry, she swung away. 'All right. What would happen if she walked through that door right now?'

'We would talk.'

'And then?' she demanded.

'It would depend on what she said.'

Grabbing a plate off the dresser, she deliberately threw it on the floor. 'And if she wanted to come back to you? What then? It would be bye-bye, Carenza?'

'I don't know. Go to bed. Please.'

'Go to bed,' she mimicked. 'Alone?'

'Alone,' he agreed. 'Don't make it harder than it already is.'

Picking up another plate, she held it in front of her. 'How many others?'

'What?'

'How many other women?'

'I don't know what you mean.'

'Yes, you do,' she cried. 'Yes, you *do*! If you're in love with Helena, how can you be attracted to me? And if you're attracted to me, how many other women have attracted you?'

'None.'

Hugging the plate to her chest, she slowly looked at him. 'None?'

'No.'

'Then tell me how…'

'I don't know how. Or why.'

'I don't accept things, Beck,' she warned. 'Not if I can change them.'

'So I'm beginning to discover.'

'Don't sound so bleak. I can't stand it.' Carefully putting the plate back, she bent down to pick up the broken pieces of china.

'Leave them.'

She ignored him. She felt as though she was going to fall apart. 'You feel about me as I feel about you,' she stated positively.

'Yes.'

'But we can't do anything about it.'

'No.'

With a rather bitter little smile, she misquoted softly, 'And I could have loved thee had I loved not honour more. Looks like Plan B, then, doesn't it?'

'Plan B?' he asked tiredly.

'Well, Plan A was seduction, a glorious—' Breaking off, she sucked in a deep, painful breath. 'Plan B is cold showers. Well, that's all right, isn't it?

Because we don't have any hot water. I hope the plate was valuable.' Without another word, she dumped the pieces of china in his hands and walked upstairs.

Groping around in the dark, she sat on the edge of the bed and shook. She had never wanted anyone as she wanted him. It was bewildering and frightening, and consequences didn't seem to matter. He hadn't answered when she'd asked if he adored Helena. Why? Because he still did? But no mention had been made of love. Not about Helena, not about herself. And how could he love her? He didn't know her any more than she knew him.

Dragging off her boots, she flung herself back on the bed, turned her head towards the door, which she could just dimly make out. She wanted it to open, for him to walk through it, naked. Rolling on to her face, she hugged the pillow hard. Eyes open, she stared at nothing. She could still feel the pressure of his mouth against hers, the damp hands against her back. There was an ache inside that no pain-killer would ever assuage.

She couldn't go on like this. As soon as the roads were open she would leave and never come back.

She should have tried to see his side of it; if she were a nice person, she would have. If she'd known what his side of it was. But she didn't feel nice, she felt betrayed. The very first time she had met him, she had wanted him for herself. Not transitory, not just sex or flirtation, but for always. Someone to grow old with.

It sounded so absurd.

What was he doing now? Sitting at the table with the horribly strong coffee that he liked? Was he thinking about her? Or about Helena. Beautiful, stupid Helena. She almost hoped she *was* dead. No, she didn't. And if she carried on at the centre, and people saw them together, no one would fail to notice how they felt about each other... How she felt about him. He was attracted to her, but that didn't mean he wanted anything more. So what did that make him? And why couldn't he even *tell* her about his relationship with Helena?

Kisses were cheap. Who'd said that? Someone— she couldn't remember. She would get up in a minute, go to the bathroom—grope to the bathroom, borrow a nightie or pyjamas. She shouldn't have lost her temper.

No other women, he'd said. Did she believe him? She didn't know. But why, why was he being so arbitrary?

When she opened her eyes, it was daylight—and the second night that she'd slept in her clothes. Rolling on to her back, she stared at the window. It was still raining. She didn't want to get up and face a new day. Didn't want the hassle of it, the ache of it.

Was he awake? Rolling to her feet, she went to stare from the window. Would there ever come a day when she would wake with him beside her? You barely know him, Carenza. But it didn't matter. Didn't make any difference at all. Hands shoved in her pockets, she continued to stare at the dripping landscape.

Turning away, she walked along to the bathroom. Pushing inside, she found a steaming kettle waiting for her. Beck must have heard her moving around. Helena didn't deserve him. She shouldn't have left. Mouth firm, determination in her eyes, she stripped off, washed, donned her own now dry underwear, dressed, and then walked downstairs.

'They've found Helena,' he informed her quietly.

Halting abruptly, all the wind taken out of her sails, the words echoed emptily in her mind. 'Where?' she demanded rustily. 'Is she…?'

'Alive? Yes. Winchester.'

'Winchester?'

'Yes.'

Unable to take it in, she sank down at the table and just stared at him.

'Coffee?'

'Yes.' She felt numb, unable to think. 'How did you…?'

'Find out? Doug just told me. Extra help has been drafted in from other stations, two from Winchester. They recognised her picture at the local station. They radioed Doug to let me know.'

'I see.' His voice had been flat, empty of meaning,

and she said waspishly, 'You don't sound very ec-static.'

'No. The council crews have been working all nigh—'

'No?' she interrupted.

'Sorry?'

'I said, You don't sound very ecstatic, and you said, "No."'

'Did I?' he asked vaguely. 'The roads should be open in a few hours. I need to go and see her, Carrie.'

'Yes.' What else could she say? Railing at him wouldn't do any good. Neither would behaving like a shrew. And he had said he wasn't happy at going to see her, so there was hope, wasn't there? Or had he really not been paying attention to what he'd been saying? Because he was numb? Overjoyed? Or hadn't even been listening to what Carrie had been saying?

He handed her her coffee, and she sat staring down into it. Bye-bye, Carrie? No, not necessarily, it depended on what she said, didn't it? 'Perhaps you could give me a lift to the nearest station.'

'I'll take you home.'

She merely nodded. Words were very hard to find. And it was all so silly. She didn't even know him. 'I came down all prepared to have a row with you,' she murmured.

'I thought that was last night.'

'That wasn't a row, that was a minor spat. You

should see me when I *really* get going.' Only now, of course, he wouldn't. 'What else did Doug say?'

'Nothing much, just that she was alive and well, and living in Winchester.'

Needing pain to ease the numbness, she asked masochistically, 'And if she'd never existed…'

'She does exist.'

She gave a humourless laugh. 'Stop being so pedantic.' After a few moments' silence, she added almost conversationally, 'I've never invited a man into my bed before. Never instigated lovemaking. Never spoken to a man as I spoke to you. I don't seem to be behaving like myself at all. I'm going for a walk.' Lurching to her feet, she grabbed her jacket off the chair.

'You haven't eaten…'

'Not hungry.' Walking out, shrugging into her jacket as she went, she lifted her face to the rain. Not so hard today, more of a drizzle really, but it would hide her tears.

Defeated before the battle had even begun. Helena must be something really, really special. There was a hard lump in her throat, a tightness in her chest.

She didn't know where she walked. Didn't care. Perhaps she should go and see Helena. And say what? Leave him alone?

She could hear a chain-saw in the distance, the sound of heavy machinery. She'd be all right once she got home. She couldn't afford not to come back and finish the conference centre, but she didn't need to come out every day. She could instruct the decorators, come down once or twice maybe... She didn't need to see him.

Would he bring Helena back with him? She couldn't even accuse him of being a rat. She'd done all the running. He'd merely been reluctantly attracted.

But why, why would he want Helena *back*? Because he loved her. Because she was special to him.

And Carrie wasn't.

Why couldn't she believe that he was the sort of man who could be attracted to two women at the same time? Maybe even more than two; she only had his word for it that he wasn't.

You're just desperate for love, Carrie. See someone, want them... No, it wasn't that. She wasn't desperate... Yes, she was. But only for him.

Feeling wretched and almost ill, she turned to walk back. An old, mud-spattered Land Rover was parked beside the house. A working vehicle. Not one of those fancy off-roaders for women who only used them to take their children to school. Beck's, she supposed. Which meant that she could go home.

Pushing open the back door, she halted. He was standing by the table. He looked incredibly contained. And good-looking of course. Much too good-looking for her peace of mind. She wanted to see him on a yacht, hair tousled by the wind, chin unshaven... Wanted to see him on a mountain...

'Ready?'

'Yes.' She picked up her pad and walked out again. And stopped. 'You still have my car keys.' She couldn't get into her flat without them. Her front-door key was also on the ring.

He handed them to her, opened the door of the Rover and waited for her to climb inside.

Closing the door, he walked round and got in beside her.

They drove away in silence. He obviously wasn't going to explain anything, tell her anything, and she was damned if she was going to ask.

The damage to the countryside was far more severe than she had expected. Staring from her window, she was horrified by the destruction. Everything that had been familiar was changed. And yet, she supposed, in a few weeks, nature would have taken over. Spring growth would hide the scars, birds and animals would recover, make new homes... And what would she be doing in a few weeks? Still be moping?

No, she determined. She would get over it. Of course she would. She didn't even know him.

The sound of the engine, accompanied by her own misery, lulled her into a sort of stupor until he spoke.

'Straight on?'

'What? Oh, yes.' She directed him to her flat and he stopped, switched off the engine.

'I'll let you know—'

'No,' she interrupted. 'You really think I want to

know that you're playing happy families with Helena? I'll finish the centre, let you have the invoice, and then...' And then nothing. She couldn't even hate him. She wished she could. Opening her door, she added quietly, 'Goodbye, Beck.'

She didn't look back, didn't even hear him drive away. She closed the door behind her and leaned against it. Over, she told herself, before it had even begun. Depending on what Helena said, of course. She might say she didn't want him, in which case...

Straightening, she idly flicked the light switch, found that she had electricity, switched on the emersion heater, and walked across to the phone. Which worked. She rang the insurance company, asked for a claim form, asked about a hire car, became briskly efficient and in no mood for incompetence. From anyone. She then rang the firm of decorators she used, explained the situation, made an appointment to meet them later that afternoon, and went to have a long soak in the bath.

By ten o'clock, she was exhausted, hungry and desolate. She forced herself to eat something, and then went to bed.

The doorbell woke her, dragged her from a deep sleep, and she lay for a moment trying to orientate herself. Glancing at the clock, she saw that it was two o'clock in the morning. Barely thinking, barely awake, she grabbed her dressing gown to cover her nakedness, and stumbled to answer the front door. Which was stupid; it could have been anyone.

It wasn't anyone. It was Beck. He looked tired, his hair all untidy as though he'd been running his hands through it.

'Can I come in?'

'No.'

'Yes.' Taking the door out of her hand, he walked in, closed it behind him and kissed her. Hard. Dragged her into his arms and kissed her as though he was never going to stop.

With a ragged breath, he finally released her. 'Coffee?' he queried. Without waiting for an answer, which was just as well because she was incapable of giving one, he walked past her to look for the kitchen. She blindly followed, eyes fixed on his back as though if she took her gaze away for an instant he would disappear.

'Do you have anything on under that robe?' he asked as he hunted in cupboards for the coffee.

'No,' she denied thickly.

'Good, because I intend to make love to you soon. Very, very soon.'

Shoving her hair off her face, she leaned weakly against the wall. 'Why not now?' She sounded strangled.

'Because I need to talk to you first, and caffeine might—just might—distract me whilst I do so.'

'Where's Helena?'

'Winchester. Do you want some?'

'No.' She watched him make his coffee, and when he turned she looked hastily down.

'Last year,' he began quietly, flatly, as though none of it mattered, it was just a story, 'I was involved in a diving accident. Someone died. Whilst I was in the hospital…'

'Hospital?' she asked sharply.

'Yes, it doesn't matter, just some head injuries,' he explained dismissively, 'broken ribs. I met Helena. She was the sister of the man who died. I blamed myself for the accident. Irrationally so, perhaps, but I did blame myself. I'd had a phone call the night before to tell me that my mother had died.' With a rather grim smile, he continued, 'It was my father who was ill, but it was my mother who died. A heart attack. Spanner always stayed with them when I was away; she'd just come back from taking him for a walk, sat in the chair, and…died. There weren't any flights out until the next evening, and so, perhaps stupidly, I agreed to make a last dive with the team before I flew home. There was nothing I could do for my mother, only grieve. It's dangerous to dive without a partner, and the team needed me. It was our last day. And I keep thinking if I hadn't gone, or if I'd done this or that, seen what was about to happen… Helena visited me every day. She was extraordinarily beautiful, and I was grateful for her visits and her lack of blame. She came with me to my mother's funeral, and I went with her to her brother's.'

'I'm sorry,' she said inadequately.

'Yes. We went to stay with my father, and I

thought he was all right. Or maybe it was only what
I wanted to believe. I don't know. I needed to go to
a London hospital for a check-up…I could have left
it, could have gone later, but I didn't. He had a nurse
with him, and I thought he was all right, or as all
right as anyone can be when they've just lost their
partner of forty-two years and they have cancer. I
would only be gone a few days. Grieving for my
mother, Helena's brother, worried about my father,
I left. He died the next day. And Helena was there
for me. Through all the tragedies, Helena was there.'

Unable to bear it, she hurried across to him and
took him in her arms.

He put down his coffee and returned the embrace.
Chin on her hair, he continued in the same quiet
voice, 'I was grateful to her.'

'And Helena? What did she feel?'

'I don't know.'

She could feel the soft thud of his heart against
her cheek, feel the warmth of him, the sadness.

'She's with someone else now.'

Leaning back, she looked up, traced his strong
jaw with her fingers. 'And so you're—free?'

'And so I'm free.' As he looked at her, the harsh
electric light put planes and angles on his face that
she hadn't noticed before. Made him appear somehow gaunt. 'I couldn't tell you all this before, until
I had made sure she was all right.'

'And is she?'

'Yes.'

'She didn't feel guilty that there had been a police investigation?'

'I don't know. I didn't ask her.'

And what else hadn't he asked her? she wondered. What else was he carefully not saying? Because there was *something*.

'Why wouldn't she have been all right?' she asked softly. 'Because she loved you? Adored you? And you couldn't return her feelings?'

'No.'

'So why did she leave without taking anything with her?'

'She hadn't been—well.'

'As in—nervous breakdown?'

'Something like that.'

'Because of you?'

The hesitation was longer this time, and then he agreed, 'Partly. I couldn't just forget her, Carrie, pretend she never existed. And I couldn't admit my attraction for you until I knew she was all right.'

'Because you felt responsible?'

'Yes.'

'And was that why her father hated you? Because his son had died, and Helena was with you?'

'Yes. He needed to blame someone. I didn't mind that it was me. Payback time,' he said softly.

'Sorry?'

'All my life, things had been—easy. Home, school, university, a job I loved. I could afford to indulge my passions for mountaineering, sailing, anything I chose. A privileged life. I knew that. And then, in the space of a few months, it all fell apart. Payback time. I thought I was dealing with everything OK. Coping, doing all the right things, but when my father died it just seemed too much. I went to stay in his house, sold my own; I thought it might make me understand. Help. It didn't. Everything felt distanced, numb. And then I met you. Such a laughing girl. Tall and competent... It came as something of a shock to find that I wanted you. That I was instantly attracted. I should have denied you the contract. I knew that.'

'So did I,' she agreed softly.

'Yes. But I told myself that by February, when you were due to start, everything would be different.' Searching her face tilted towards his own, he gently traced one finger down her cheek, gave a faint smile when she shivered. 'And then Helena left and I was angry because she'd left in such a way that I couldn't get on with my life. And February seemed such a long way away. You said that you used to watch for me walking in the grounds. I used to watch for you too. Each morning I would wait for you to arrive. Catch a glimpse of you through a window. All quick smiles and warm brown eyes. Vital one minute, thoughtful the next. If the tree hadn't fallen on you...' With a quick smile of his own, he added, 'You didn't play by the rules, Carenza. You weren't supposed to tell me how you felt.'

'You knew how I felt. I can't hide things.'

'No. I'm sorry. The last thing I ever wanted to do was hurt you.'

'Then don't hurt me now.'

'I don't intend to.'

Body melting at the look in his eyes, heart thudding as he untied her belt and slipped his hands inside to touch her warm flesh, she shuddered, grasped frantically at his damp jacket. His kiss was—devastating.

With a long groan of need, she kissed him back, worried at his mouth as though she might lose this for ever. He grunted as her teeth bit into his lower lip and pulled her hard against him. His hands were everywhere. Shaping her, touching her, feeling her, arousing, and she pressed tighter, tighter, almost mindless in her need for him.

He scooped her up, eventually found the bedroom, and laid her on the tumbled bed. Stripping off, his eyes on hers, he joined her, pulled her once more against him.

'Are you on the Pill?'

'Yes.'

'Promise?'

'Promise. Don't talk any more.'

Feverish was perhaps the best description of their first lovemaking. Feverish and urgent, and incredibly skilful on his part. He brought her body alive, made it sing and cry out for more.

His mouth roved over every part she wanted it to

rove, her hands shaped every muscle and contour of his hard body. They didn't speak, just indulged in pleasure and excitement and unbelievable need. His mouth was driving her crazy. Never still, he touched every inch of her, fulfilling desires she'd never known she had. And if the bed had been tumbled before it was now a complete and utter mess. Struggling to untangle one foot from the duvet, she dragged his mouth back to hers and rolled to cover him. Her breathing ragged, as though she'd been running for ever, she lifted her head and stared down into his grey eyes. Sleepy eyes, eyes full of dark desire with lashes to die for. Her mouth felt bruised, her eyes barely focused, her face flushed, and her heart wasn't coping at all well.

He framed her face, stared at her for long, long moments of intensity. 'Do you know how long I've wanted to do that?'

'As long as I've wanted you to?'

He smiled. A slow, warm, incredibly sexy smile. A smile to break hearts. She had never seen him smile like that, and found her own mouth curving in response.

'If you had felt anything like I felt staying in your house, well, all I can say is that you must have terrific self-control.'

'A control that was tested to the limit. You fit very nicely into my arms, Miss Dean.'

'That's because I was made for you. Specially for you. And now, after all the turmoil, I feel safe, and languid, and loved,' she told him softly. No words could describe what had just happened. Nothing would ever come close. He was beautiful, and exciting, and she loved him. She wasn't going to ask him if he loved her. She was going to savour the moment, hold it close for ever. Remember that heaven could be found. It could.

He gently rolled her to the side, carefully untangled the duvet, and leaned over her. He touched his mouth to hers once, twice, and then a third time for a lingering, slow kiss that curled her toes. Feeling lethargic and satiated, she slid her hands slowly across his back. Revelled in the feeling of fingertips on warm flesh. His mouth moved to her neck, and she moaned with pleasure, snuggled more warmly against him.

It was just getting light when they finally slipped into sleep. Curled together, faces close, bodies relaxed, they slept until gone nine, and only woke then because someone was leaning on the doorbell.

With a quick smile, she found her robe and went to answer it.

'The hire car,' she explained when she came back. 'Coffee?'

'Not yet,' he denied as he held his hand out to her. When she reached him, he pulled her down beside him and snuggled her against his warm body. 'Where shall we go?'

'Go?'

'Mm. Paris, Rome, Vienna…'

'Work?'

He gave his slow smile. 'I'll give you the day off.'

'Can't. I have to meet the decorators. Yesterday, after you brought me home, I told them it needed to be finished quickly.'

'I hurt you yesterday,' he said sombrely. 'I won't hurt you any more.'

'Good.'

'I need a shave.'

She smiled. 'Just have to be careful kissing me, then, won't you?'

'Mm. Take your robe off. You have a beautiful body and I want to see all of it.'

'It's a very large body. I'm a big girl,' she informed him just in case he hadn't noticed.

'With a big heart.'

'And a temper.'

'Yes, and a temper. But the plate wasn't valuable.'

'Good.'

It was nearly midday when they were ready to leave. 'I'll see you at the centre.'

'No,' she denied as she slid her arms round his neck and gave him one last kiss. 'Come and see me tonight. I have lots of things to do today.' Hesitating a moment, she added seriously, 'Don't tell John about us.'

'Why?'

'I don't know. Call it feminine intuition.'

He looked puzzled, but she couldn't tell him that

she didn't think John would be very pleased, that he
would expect Beck and Helena to get back together.
And she didn't want this spoilt. She had a horrible
feeling it would be, if John found out.

CHAPTER FIVE

'SORRY I'm late,' she apologised to the decorators. 'Had to wait for the hire car.' With a warm smile, she laid out her sketches for reference, made sure they had all the materials they required, and disappeared to consult with the curtain maker and collect the wallpaper and other fittings. She had never felt so happy.

Beck was waiting for her when she got back to her flat at gone seven.

'I'll need a key,' he said softly as he kissed her hello and presented her with a very large bunch of roses.

'I'll get one cut. Thank you,' she added as she inhaled the scent of the flowers. She couldn't keep the smile from her face, couldn't stop touching him. Small, intimate gestures, fingers to his face, his arm, holding his hand against her mouth.

'Make love to me.'

'I was intending to.' Taking the roses from her, he laid them on the hall table, and ushered her into the bedroom.

They ate out, very late, and went back to bed.

The next day was the same, except that he came into the centre. Against her strict instructions. With a secret little smile that she wasn't aware of, she walked into the annexe where there would be privacy.

'Go away,' she told him softly as she wrapped her arms round his neck. 'I'm busy.'

'You're beautiful.'

'I'm a troll.'

He laughed and bent his head to kiss her. 'You're very addictive, Miss Dean.'

'I'm also very busy, and happy, and I don't want anyone to know. I want to keep it private and special. Hug it to myself. Come and see me tonight.'

'Certainly. Tomorrow and Saturday, I will be late.'

'I know.'

'You could stay at the house.'

'No.' She didn't want to explain that she didn't want to make love to him in a house where he'd made love to Helena. 'Come to the flat. You don't mind driving back and forth?'

'No.' His eyes were full of laughter. It was so good to see.

Rubbing her finger along his bottom lip, she whispered, 'I like to see you smile.'

'I like to see you naked.'

'And me. You, I mean. Go away,' she laughed. 'You're confusing me.'

'Arousing.'

'Yes, and one of my workmen is coming.' He

stepped away and ran one hand over the newly plastered wall. 'Slight bump here, I think.'

'No, there isn't.'

He gave the workman a bland smile, and walked out. She laughed and wanted to keep on laughing.

That evening he brought her a crystal—'For happiness,' he explained—and the next a packet of strong French coffee. 'For me.'

By the end of the week she had a small china rabbit that he constantly moved 'in case he gets bored', a set of drawing pencils and a rag doll because she was the last one in the shop and she looked sad.

'Her name's Polly.'

'Right.' Eyes full of laughter and love, she hugged him hard.

The following week she took two days off and they flew to Venice. In his private plane.

'I didn't know you had one.'

'You don't know a lot of things,' he said simply. 'I also have a yacht. Well,' he qualified, 'dinghy. And I only have a quarter share in the plane.'

'Cheapskate.'

She had never felt happier or more fulfilled. He was a delight. They held hands as they walked through museums and art galleries, did all the silly, touristy things that lovers do. They ate by candlelight, made love by moonlight, and every minute in his company she fell deeper and deeper in love. She would have died for him. She had never known that someone could come to mean so much. He was funny and serious, spoke fluent Italian and French, and his wry self-mockery delighted her. So did the fact that other women watched him hungrily, with desire in their eyes.

'What do you do during the day?' she asked curiously as they drove back to her flat.

'Catch up on my sleep.'

'No, seriously,' she laughed. 'With the restaurant only open three days, don't you get bored?'

'*Bored?* I've never been bored in my life.'

'Then what do you do?' she persisted.

'Write.'

'Sorry?'

'Write,' he repeated. 'Articles on mountaineering, archaeology…'

'Published?'

'Mm-hmm.'

'I'm impressed.'

'Good. Can I tell anyone yet?'

Cautious, she asked, 'Like who?'

'Like everyone. People aren't fools, and a Cheshire-cat grin on my face, whistling while I work…'

'Do you?' she asked, intrigued.

'Do I what?'

'Whistle.'

He laughed. 'Carrie, Carrie, what am I to do with you? You're my utter delight and we can't keep it a secret.'

Sobering, she asked quietly, 'Did you? With Helena?'

'No, and I don't want to talk about Helena.'

'What did she do?'

'Do?' he asked somewhat cautiously, she thought.

'Mm, job, employment, whatever. Those clothes in her wardrobe didn't come cheap.'

'Oh, I don't think she did anything. Her mother left her some money, I believe.'

And when she was with Beck she lived off him? 'Did you buy her the clothes?'

'Carrie,' he warned quietly. 'It's none of your business.'

'No. Sorry. Do you still think about her?'

'No.' Pulling up outside her flat, he switched off the engine and turned to face her. 'I like you very much. I want to be with you all the time, not only in snatches. I want everyone to know that my—happiness isn't because Helena's been found.'

'And is that what everyone assumes?'

'Yes.' Gently tucking her hair back behind her ears, stroking down the thick length of it, he smiled at her. 'The last eight months have been so wretched, so full of grief. Helena's brother, my parents, Spanner...'

'I'm sorry.' Resting her head against his shoulder, she smoothed one hand against his back, wondered, before hastily dismissing the thought, whether his happiness was just a natural reaction to that grief. And that when he was whole again... 'I know I'm being selfish,' she said softly. 'It's just that... Oh, I don't know, it's been so good, Beck, I didn't want to share.' Looking up, she smiled at him, gently kissed his mouth. 'You're a very special person. Very special.'

'No.'

'Yes. I don't know what it is about you, but you make people feel safe.'

'That's silly.'

'No, it isn't. People watch you, defer to you, as though they *know* you're different.'

'Oh, Carrie, I'm not different.'

'You are, but I don't know how to explain it. And I'm very afraid that I'll lose you. That this is borrowed time.'

'All time is borrowed,' he said softly. 'Losing my parents brought that home to me. I wish you could have met them.'

'I wish I had too. Did they know Helena?'

'My father met her, but he was lost in his own grief. He left me a letter...'

Hugging him again, only a small comfort, she knew, because only time would ease his pain, she pressed her mouth to his neck. 'What did he say?'

'That he was sorry. That I mustn't blame myself for not being there. But I do, Carrie. I do. And that he loved me, was proud of me... It hurts. They were both good people. Are your parents still alive?'

'Yes, they live in Devon. You'll like them—I like them, anyway,' she grinned. 'My brother lives in

New Zealand. He's small, and slim. We got the wrong bodies.'

'No,' he corrected, 'the right bodies. I like big girls. Handy for pulling up sails, hauling in the anchor...'

'Shall I?'

'I hope so.'

'I'll like that.'

'Good.'

They smiled at each other, a long smile, eyes holding, and finally went inside. She knew that he was keeping part of himself separate from her, and assumed that it was because he wasn't sure about his feelings for her, but it hurt, that little exclusion zone, made her feel less confident. But, despite that, over the next few days it became harder and harder to keep their affair secret. He would *persist* in coming over to the centre, ostensibly to make sure everything was on schedule, in reality, to steal precious moments of her time. Which, of course, delighted her.

On the Friday afternoon, she was up on the stepladder hanging the curtains in the lounge area of the centre when he came in. She turned to give him a quick smile over her shoulder, then yelped in alarm when he climbed up the ladder behind her.

'Beck! Someone will see!'

'The decorators are all in the extension,' he informed her smugly. 'I checked. Let me do that; you shouldn't be standing on top of the ladder.'

'It's my job.'

'No,' he denied smoothly, 'your job is to make me happy. Hello,' he added all in the same breath as he kissed her.

'Get off,' she laughed. 'You'll have us both off.'

'Then come over to the house.'

'No.'

He jumped down and lifted her off and into his arms. 'There's something I want to discuss with you.'

'Discuss it here.'

'No, we might be interrupted. I haven't seen you for hours.'

'You saw me this morning.'

'You're a hard woman.'

'I'm a working woman.'

Hands to either side of her face, he stared down at her, his eyes dark. 'God, I want you.'

That alarming, delightful dip in her tummy, her own face sobering, she whispered, 'I want you too.'

'Then come over to the house.' Without giving her a chance to refuse, he caught her hand and pulled her out through the open door. Breaking into a run so that she was forced to do likewise or fall over, laughing, they ran across the grounds and into the house.

They didn't see John watching them, didn't see anything at all. Didn't even feel the cold wind. He opened the back door, tugged her inside and into his arms. Walking her backwards towards the sitting room, eyes on her face, he toppled her down on to the sofa that had been pulled in front of the fire.

'The stage already set?' she teased.

'Of course.' Lying on top of her, staring down into her warm brown eyes, elbows taking his weight, he slowly kissed her.

'No doubts that you could get me here?'

'None. And I want you naked. Don't squirm,' he warned her huskily.

'I have to squirm. It's what you make me do.' Burrowing her hands beneath his sweater, she untucked his shirt so that she could reach the warm flesh of his back. 'You didn't lock the back door.'

'No one will come.'

'Such confidence,' she mocked. Her voice was thick, husky. 'Draw the curtains.'

'I don't want to move.'

'Oh, Beck.' Tilting back her head, she accepted his mouth as though she was starving, and the crazy dance began all over again. Neither saw the face at the window as they undressed each other; both were too involved to care if they had.

Lying naked, warmly entwined in the darkening room, the fire flickering across them, they made love with a slow, exciting languor that left them drained and content.

'I find it truly amazing,' he said softly as he stroked her hair back from her face, 'that you make me feel so much. I think about you all the time, you know. Wonder about you, imagine what you might be doing.'

'So do I. I want to know all there is to know about you; want to touch you all the time. Feel you move inside me. It's scary and wonderful and it's taking over my life.'

He kissed her again, slow and lingering, and she couldn't get enough. Couldn't get close enough, near enough, couldn't even begin to articulate what she felt for him. How he could make her feel.

Stroking his warm back, feeling sleepy and content, she examined his strong face, the beautiful eyes that could make her heart race, the mouth that could elicit such amazing responses. 'I should go back,' she murmured without conviction. 'I have to finish hanging the curtains.'

'Finish them tomorrow.'

'Tomorrow's Saturday.'

'I know it's... Oh, my God, what's the time?' Grabbing his watch off the floor, he held it out to the flames in order to see it, then leapt to his feet. 'The restaurant opens in an hour.' Naked as the day he was born, he ran out, and she heard him running up the stairs, the soft slam of a door.

Laughing, she hugged the cushion to herself, and was still there when he came down ten minutes later. Hair wet, shaved, just wearing his whites, he stared at her and shook his head. 'I'll see you later,' he said hastily. 'Are you staying?'

'No.'

'I can put out an extra place at the restaurant...'

'No,' she denied softly.

He gave her a look of disgust. 'You can't hide for ever.'

'I know.'

'Then put the guard in front of the fire when you leave. I have to go.' And he was gone.

No, she couldn't hide for ever. Just for a while longer. Getting slowly to her feet, she stretched like a cat, bundled up her clothes and went up to have a shower.

It was gone two when he arrived at the flat, and she was waiting, his coffee percolating, the bed invitingly turned down.

'You're spoiling me,' he said softly as he took her in his arms.

'Yes, I want to,' she said seriously. Head tipped back, her hair fell in a long brown curtain almost to her waist. 'I want to do everything for you. I can't get enough of you.' Tracing his mouth, his cheekbones, with gentle fingers, she added with a bewilderment that she knew he felt as well, 'I can't concentrate, can't think, just continually anticipate our next meeting. The thought of you makes me smile and ache. The sight of you sends me into turmoil.' And she was so very afraid that it couldn't last. They'd made no plans, just lived day by day, as though neither of them wanted to mention a future that might not be. She didn't know why he might feel that way, only knew that she did.

Eyes searching her face, as hers were searching his, he said quietly, 'Let's go to bed.'

In the morning, her fears seemed silly. 'I'll follow you down.'

'I'll take you. Seems daft to take two cars.'

'Sensible,' she corrected. 'You have to work to-night.'

'So? I can run you home first.'

'No.'

'Yes.'

'No,' she laughed. Snatching up her keys, she led the way out.

He followed her to the centre and insisted on putting up the curtains himself. Amiably arguing over the right and the wrong way to do it, neither heard the car arrive. Their backs to the door, neither was aware of being watched until a small, soft voice intruded.

'Beck?'

He stilled, and his face changed. All expression was suddenly wiped away as though with a cloth. Lowering the curtain he was holding, he slowly turned. So did Carrie.

'Oh, Beck.' Like a little girl, lost and sad, blue eyes full of tears, Helena ran into his arms with no expectation of being rejected. As she wasn't.

'It's today,' she said tearfully.

'Is it?' His voice was emotionless.

'Yes. Did you forget?'

'Yes,' he sighed.

Standing stock-still, Carrie watched them until Helena lifted her head from Beck's shoulder, and looked at her. She gave a weary smile. 'Would you excuse us for a little while?'

'Yes, of course.' Her own voice a masterly impression of wood, Carrie turned and walked away into the extension. She felt as though she'd been smacked. What was today? she wondered numbly. Some sort of anniversary? Hands shoved into her pockets, she stared blindly out at the small patio area. Beck had always said he liked her size, and she'd laughingly called herself a troll. Tiny, exquisite Helena made her feel like one.

She hadn't stood here deliberately in order to watch for them emerging, but she had a very good view of them as they walked to a small blue car. Beck had his arm round her shoulders.

'Who's the blonde?'

With a little start, she turned to stare at one of the decorators. 'An old friend of Mr Beckford's,' she said quietly.

'Now why don't I have old friends like that?' he grinned.

'I don't know,' she denied listlessly.

'You all right?' he asked in concern.

'Yes, I'm fine. Just thinking. I didn't know you were working today.

'Only this morning. Thought I might as well finish that end room.'

She nodded, didn't even hear him walk away.

Don't assume, she cautioned herself. Don't even think. As soon as the blue car had gone, she returned to the lounge and finished hanging the curtains. She then drove home. How fortunate she'd brought her own car. Must have known.

She spent the rest of the day trying not to think about it, and failed miserably. She had no confidence at all in her ability to think positively. He didn't love Helena; he'd said so. But she had some sort of hold over him, didn't she? Perhaps today was the anniversary of her nervous breakdown.

Don't be bitchy.

Closing her eyes in defeat, she flung herself into the chair in the lounge. He wants you, Carenza, he told you so. Yes. So why couldn't she snap out of this apathy? This feeling of doom?

Picking up Polly, she held her in front of her, stared at the painted face. 'He does want me, Polly, and when he comes—if he comes...' He would come. Of course he would. And say—what? That Helena needed him? Tossing the doll to one side, she got up to pace restlessly. You're being extremely foolish, Carenza. You don't usually suffer from lack of confidence. No. And don't attack him when he arrives, just wait for an explanation.

With a growl of disgust for her own behaviour, she snatched up her bag and went out. She spent the evening sitting in the cinema. She didn't know what the movie was, had absolutely no idea at all, except that it featured an alien in a black rubber suit.

She made herself scrambled egg on toast when she got in, and then threw most of it away. Only a few more hours to wait. It seemed like for ever. Listening for him, waiting for him, she still jumped when she heard his key in the door. She didn't go to greet him, just stayed where she was in the lounge. Standing, arms folded across her chest, she faced the door, and waited.

He looked tired. She wanted desperately to go to him, hold him, but she couldn't.

'Don't look like that,' he reproved quietly.

'How should I look? Is she staying?'

'For a while. Carrie…'

'Did you sleep with her?'

'No,' he denied with irritating patience. 'I know you're hurting. I know you don't understand…'

'Then make me. What does she want from you?'

'Understanding,' he sighed. 'Comfort.'

'For how long?'

'I don't know.'

'I'll make you a coffee,' she said abruptly.

'Carrie…'

Pushing past him, she walked into the kitchen. She was aware of him following her, aware of him standing behind her in the doorway. 'Did you tell her about us?'

'Yes.'

Well, that was something. 'And what did she say?'

'Nothing.'

'*Nothing?*' she demanded in disbelief as she swung round to face him. 'An ex-lover comes back to you wanting…whatever she wanted, and you tell her that you are involved with someone else, and she says *nothing*?'

'No.'

Turning back to her task, she said flatly, 'It's only instant.'

'I expected tears,' he commented quietly. 'Pleas for reassurance. You don't want them?'

'No,' she denied stonily. 'Yes.'

She felt him move, and then his hands were on her shoulders. 'Nothing's changed.'

'Hasn't it?' she asked sadly.

'No.'

'But she's living in your house…'

'For a while.'

'Does she know you're here?'

'Yes.'

'I bet she didn't break a plate.'

'No.' Slowly turning her, he looked down into her sad face. 'Stop making it harder for yourself.' Gently rubbing his thumb along her lower lip, he watched what he was doing, and then he bent his head and kissed her. A long, slow, hungry kiss that only intensified her despair. Clinging tightly, she kissed him back with a desperation she hated herself for.

'I can't bear to lose you,' she whispered.

'You haven't lost me,' he reassured her.

'I thought she had someone else,' she murmured in a small voice.

'So did I. I don't need this, Carrie. I don't want it, but...'

'But?'

Holding her against him, his cheek resting on her hair, he explained heavily, 'But today—yesterday,' he corrected, 'was the date given for the baby's birth.'

CHAPTER SIX

EYES snapping open, she shoved herself away. *'Baby?'* she squeaked. 'What baby?' She couldn't have been more shocked if he'd slapped her.

'Helena was having a baby…our baby,' he qualified just in case the point might have escaped her. 'She miscarried. Last October.'

Barely able to find her voice, she husked, 'That was why…'

'She had the breakdown, yes. Why I had to find her. Why I'm allowing her to stay in my house.'

Unable to think straight, unable to take it all in, she stepped away from him and shoved her hands through her hair.

'It was a boy,' he added quietly.

'You wanted it,' she said jerkily.

'Yes. After all the tragedy, the grief, it seemed the one bright thing in the world. Something to look forward to. A new family.'

'But you didn't love her.'

'I was—fond of her. I thought we would be able to make a good life together after the initial shock,' he added honestly.

'Which was why you got engaged.'

He sighed. 'We didn't, actually, get engaged. But we were going to be married.'

'Until she lost the baby.'

'Yes.'

'Which was why you made me promise that I was on the Pill,' she stated. 'I should feel pity for her, anguish, but I don't. That's not very nice, is it? But I only feel it for you. If you wanted the baby...' Taking a deep breath, her back to him, she ran her hand over the cool surface of the worktop. 'I don't know what to say. Or think. Why didn't you tell me this before?'

'She didn't want it known.'

'And so you feel responsible for her.'

'Yes.'

And the stupid thing was, she thought, that she wouldn't have liked him half so well if he *hadn't* had such a sense of responsibility. 'And so you have two women in your life, and they're both giving you grief.'

When he didn't answer, she turned. The look on his face hurt her unbearably. Going to him, she put her arms round him and rested her head against his chest. 'I'm sorry, I'm being utterly selfish. You won't expect us to be friends, will you?'

He gave a small smile and kissed the top of her head. 'No, Carrie, I won't expect you to be friends.'

'And she'll get better, won't she? Go off and find new chums for herself, another man...'

'Yes.'

But supposing she didn't? Supposing she continued to cling? What then? And if it eventually, finally, came to a choice, who would he choose?

Lifting her head, she gave him an uncertain smile. 'Come to bed. It's late, and you're tired.'

Taking his hand, as though he were a child, she led him into the bedroom and undressed him. Tucking him under the covers, ignoring the wry smile in his eyes, she undressed and climbed in beside him.

'I don't need a mother figure, Carrie,' he said drily.

'I know, but you do need some fun in your life, don't you?'

And she did try very hard to make it fun, but both knew she failed. Something was missing, something was different. His mind wasn't exclusively on her, and hers kept wandering to thoughts of Helena. When he finally fell asleep, she lay and watched him. So good-looking, so impossibly good-looking, and the odd thing was, he wasn't in the least conceited. He was just—Beck. She didn't know if he had a temper, didn't know what made him laugh, and if she gave him grief about this she would never find out. She would lose him. She had to be understanding, kind… Put herself in Helena's place. How would she have felt in the same position? Desolate, and she'd fight tooth and nail to keep him. As any sane woman would. But no matter how frustrated, or despairing, or angry, he might feel he wasn't going to talk about Helena to her. Wasn't going to deride her, complain about her; that wasn't his way. He felt responsible, and perhaps guilty that he didn't love her… Did Helena love him? Hard to see how she couldn't. But she *had* left him. Perhaps she had tried to make the break, put her life in order, and then, when the anniversary came up, needed Beck to be with her. She'd lost her brother… Be charitable, Carenza.

With a deep sigh, she lay down, but she couldn't sleep. And the thought that he had made love to Helena made her feel sick. She had *known* they were lovers, or had assumed so, but tangible proof, as in a baby, was somehow different. Knowing Helena was in his house made it different. She didn't know the other woman; she might be a sweet, gentle person who needed understanding and help. Why couldn't she believe that? Because she didn't want to? Because she needed to hate her?

Rather disturbed because she had thought she had a nicer nature than that, she turned over, tried to capture sleep. If she rubbished Helena, she would lose. If she was nice about Helena, would she still lose? She needed to know what she was like. Know what Beck really thought about her. Know thine enemy. But she wasn't an enemy, was she?

They woke late the next morning within moments of each other, and then just lay looking into each other's face. 'All right?' he asked gently.

'Yes. Beck?'

'Mm?'

'I need to know what she's like,' she blurted.

His face went all still and quiet, and she didn't know if he was angry, or just thinking. But she did need to know.

'I don't know what she's like,' he finally admitted. 'She isn't like you.'

'And is that good, or bad?' she asked, trying for some humour.

'Good.' Releasing one arm from the covers, he touched his fingers to her face as though he needed contact, and she snuggled against him, wrapped her legs against his. 'I'm not very good at sharing my feelings; I don't think men are. I tend to keep things to myself, cope, deal with them, but Helena seemed to assume that we needed to comfort each other, and maybe we did. Apart from my injuries, the immobility, which was driving me insane, I felt guilty about her brother.'

'But you said it wasn't your fault.'

'No, but I was with him. He'd joined the trip at the last moment, and although I'd met him on and off over the past few years, liked him, considered him a friend, I'd never actually dived with him. He said he was experienced, and certainly he *seemed* competent. We'd been down several times without incident. We were exploring an old wreck off the Falkland Islands, finding artefacts, bringing them up for examination. There were four of us diving in pairs...'

'And you were with him?'

He shook his head. 'But I was the most experienced. The wreck was unstable, we all knew that,
and we were being careful. But I keep wondering,
was my mind more on my mother than on what I
was doing? I don't really know what happened; perhaps Mike saw something he wanted, tugged on
something he shouldn't have, or maybe it would
have gone anyway. I don't know if I felt it move,
saw something, but I sent my own partner up, swam
to the others, sent Lorcan away—and the whole
thing just collapsed on top of Mike and myself.'

He was silent so long, perhaps reliving it, that she
thought he wasn't going to continue, and then he
added, 'Lorcan and Nikko came back, got us both
out, but Mike was already dead. Unconscious, I was
airlifted to the nearest hospital and when I came
round two days later it was to find Helena by my
bed.'

'And was that the first time you'd met her?'

'Yes. She was the one who told me about Mike.
She already knew about my mother. There was no
blame in her face, Carrie, only compassion.'

'When I was released, we spent a few days in a
hotel before flying home. We were booked into separate rooms, but...'

'Yes,' she agreed, 'but.' She didn't want the details of their lovemaking.

'A few weeks after my father's funeral, she told
me she thought she was pregnant. She moved with
me to my parents' house because I felt a need to be

there. She had it redecorated, I refurbished the restaurant, and then she miscarried. She was different after that…'

'And you felt responsible.'

'Yes. She was distant, irrational, wouldn't let me touch her, comfort her—and then I met you.'

'And I wasn't distant, was I? Nor unapproachable.'

'No.'

No. So perhaps what he felt for her was just relief at normality.

'I felt so guilty,' he continued. 'Ashamed. Helena had lost the baby and all I could think about was you. Not very nice behaviour, was it?'

But understandable. If Helena was being irrational, then Carrie had represented sanity. Something he desperately needed. And when this was all over and he had time to stop and stare, look around him, would he realise that he didn't need Carrie either? She didn't know why she was having this crisis of confidence, but she couldn't shake the feeling that fate hadn't finished with either of them.

He was wealthy and successful, could probably have any woman he chose. And when Helena left, if she left, and he went back to his normal life, because she didn't think the restaurant would satisfy him for ever, what then?

'That was why you stopped travelling, wasn't it?' she asked quietly. 'Opened the restaurant?'

'Yes. I couldn't go gallivanting all over the place

with a baby on the way. They would need stability, a proper home. I have to go soon.'

With a little blink, she smiled at him. 'Yes, you have lunches today. Will I see you later?'

'Do you want to?'

'Yes. I always want to see you.'

'Then I'll be back about six.'

Leaning up, she slid her hands over his warm chest, gently nuzzled her face against his, and then hid her face in his shoulder because she could feel tears forming and she didn't want him to see. It felt like goodbye, which was silly, because he hadn't intimated anything of the sort. Lips against his neck, she began to kiss him, felt his own arms come round her to hold her close. Rolling her on to her back, he searched her face, and then kissed her. Softly, gently, and then with more and more urgency until it was all she could think of. They made love almost with desperation, and when it was over he framed her face with his palms, stared deep into her eyes. 'Don't slip away from me,' he said quietly. 'It will be all right.'

'Trust me, I'm a doctor?' she quipped shakily.

'Mm.'

Finding a smile, she traced his mouth with her finger. 'I'll go and make the coffee.'

Over the next few days Helena stayed between them. They did all the things they normally did, but it was as though the stuffing had gone out of everything. And she still couldn't shake that feeling of doom.

She didn't know what happened between himself and Helena, because he didn't ever say, but it didn't stop her imagination working overtime. And then, when Beck had gone off somewhere for supplies for the restaurant, Helena came into the centre. In one of the upstairs rooms hanging curtains, Carrie saw her arrive, and the feeling of doom increased.

She heard her heels tap-tapping on the wooden stairs, and then silence as she presumably crossed the landing carpet, but she knew the exact moment the other woman arrived in the doorway of the bedroom, and slowly turned to face her. She was even prettier than Carrie remembered. But it wasn't a beauty that would last, she thought spitefully, and was immediately ashamed of herself for the thought. She was also very elegant and assured. A long woollen skirt and jacket, chunky-heeled boots, immaculate make-up. Carenza felt like a tramp in comparison.

'Hello,' she said lamely.

Helena smiled and leaned elegantly in the doorway. 'You do realise, don't you,' she asked softly, 'that he's only on loan? I mean, I don't *blame* you; he is, after all, devastatingly attractive. And wealthy. You did know he was wealthy?'

Carrie didn't answer.

'And although he says he doesn't *love* me he

won't ever be quite rid of me. We have a bond, he and I.'

'But you don't love him.'

'No. And you don't understand that, do you? But then, big girls probably don't have the perception of—dainty girls.'

'Is that right?'

'I think so.'

'I'm sorry you lost the baby.'

She lowered her lashes, long lashes, probably real. 'Yes, it was rather sad.'

'And is that really why you came back?'

'Oh, no,' she denied honestly. 'I came because of you.'

'I see. And how did you know about me?'

'John,' she said simply. 'He saw you together. Naked,' she added with a sly smile. 'Poor John was quite shocked. He's in love with me, you know.'

'Is he?'

'Oh, yes. Quite understandable of course. Have you met his wife?'

'No.'

'So plain, poor thing.'

'And has John always known where you were?' she asked carefully.

She merely smiled. Straightening, she waggled her fingers. 'Bye.'

Slumping against the wall, Carrie listened to the retreating footsteps. Was she for *real*? People didn't behave like that. They just *didn't*. Like a child playing grown-up. And she looked so *young*. She couldn't have been more than twenty-one, two. Beck was thirty-five. A little frown in her eyes, she turned to look through the window and watched Helena tippy-toe across the gravel towards the drive. She didn't act like a woman who'd had a breakdown. Not that Carrie was sure what a person who'd had a breakdown acted like—but not bitchy, surely? It was almost as though she were playing a game. She didn't even seem upset about the baby.

Chewing her lip, her frown deeper, she tried to figure out why on earth someone would want to play games. For fun? Because she was *stupid*? Or only artful? How did she behave with Beck? Or John? Not like that, that was for sure. But both men had been taken in by her, hadn't they? And Beck was far from a fool. John, she wasn't so sure about. But, if she told Beck about the encounter, and she didn't behave like that with him, she was going to look spiteful, wasn't she?

With one of the sudden decisions that was so characteristic of her, she abandoned the curtains and ran lightly down the stairs. Striding along the drive towards the gatehouse, she replayed the little conversation over and over in her head.

She heard squeals first, childish laughter, and as she rounded the bend stopped to smile at the sight of two little children playing in a mud puddle. They were absolutely filthy. Dressed identically in blue wellingtons and slickers, miniature sou'westers on their heads, they were having the time of their lives. She'd like children like that one day. Children by Beck. How remote was that possibility? she wondered.

Glancing up, she saw a woman standing in the window of the gatehouse, watching her. Lisa? Only one way to find out.

Opening the gate and carefully shutting it behind her, she walked in and knocked on the door. It was opened almost immediately. About Carenza's own age, fair hair tied back at her nape, her face was illuminated by a warm smile.

'You must be Carenza.'

'Yes. Lisa?'

'That's me. Come in.'

'Thank you.'

'I've wanted to meet you,' she said shyly as she led the way into the kitchen. 'I didn't quite like to come up to the centre.'

'I don't see why,' Carrie said wryly. 'Everyone else does.'

She giggled. 'Yes, I just saw her. Do you mind if we sit in here? I need to keep an eye on the imps.'

Shaking her head, Carrie sat herself down at the pine table. 'They're having a lovely time.'

'As you were, until she showed up? Sorry,' she apologised awkwardly.

'No need to be. Me, I'm all for plain speaking. It saves a lot of hassle. I take it you don't like her either.'

'No.' Putting on the kettle, she got out cups and saucers. 'John thinks he's in love with her,' she added with a bluntness that she obviously thought disguised her hurt.

'Then we must change his thinking,' Carenza said simply. 'She obviously doesn't behave to the men as she behaves to women.'

'No. And I can't make up my mind if she's just stupid, clever, or artful. She doesn't seem to have a conscience, or see anything wrong in what she does. And that's dangerous. Do you have milk and sugar?'

'Both, please.'

'And because I'm plain…'

'No, you aren't,' Carrie interrupted. 'And you have the loveliest smile.'

Lisa paused, turned to look at her in surprise. 'Do I?'

'Yes. John must have told you…'

Lisa lowered her eyes, gave a little sigh. 'Not lately, no. I thought everything was all right between us now, but…'

'So what are we going to do about it?' Carrie asked practically.

Lisa looked back at her, stared at her for a long, long time, and then she gave a slow smile of appreciation. 'What can we do?'

'Don't know, but I have no intention of standing around to be robbed by a baby.'

'She's twenty-eight.'

Shocked, she exclaimed, 'But that's only a year younger than I am!'

'And two years younger than me.'

They looked at each other, both clearly thinking the same thing, and laughed.

'Do you think Beck would go and look at what moisturiser she uses if I asked him nicely?' Lisa mused.

'Or vitamins. Secret formulas...' They laughed again and Lisa handed her her tea.

'Are you in love with him?'

'Yes,' Carrie agreed simply. 'I've never felt like this about a man before. I feel...' Unable to describe how she felt, she sipped her tea instead.

'I used to feel that way about John,' she confessed sadly.

'Used?'

'Yes. It all went a bit wrong.'

'I'm sorry.'

'Yes, but I've never seen Beck so happy. Laughing and joking with the staff, eager to be away each night after the restaurant closes. He comes to see you?'

'Yes.'

'So what do we do?'

'I don't know. Yet. We need a way of spiking her guns, showing them what she's really like.'

'Sounds awfully underhanded,' Lisa murmured dubiously. 'I'm not very good at intrigue.'

'But you do agree that her behaviour isn't, well, normal?'

'Yes. She's absolutely charming to John. Defers to him, smiles at him... And the people in the town, women as well as men. Everyone thinks she's wonderful.'

Except herself and Lisa. Thoughtfully sipping her tea, Carrie finally asked, 'Who was the man she was with in Winchester? Do you know? Beck said she'd found someone else.'

'I've no idea.'

'Could you ask John?'

'John?' she asked in surprise.

'Yes, he was the one who told her about me,' she explained gently. 'I think he knew where she was all along.'

'And didn't *tell* anyone?' she demanded in shock. 'No, I don't believe that! Not when everyone was so worried about her. The police even dug up Beck's garden!'

'I know.' But John had said, 'She'll come back,' really quite positively. And although Helena had only smiled when Carrie had asked her if John had known where she was all the time she'd taken it as an affirmative. She might have been wrong, of course, but she didn't think so.

Finishing her tea, she got to her feet. 'I'd better get back to the centre. If you find out anything...'

'Yes, of course,' Lisa agreed worriedly. 'Maybe she'll just go away again.'

'Maybe.' But Carenza doubted it. 'Thanks for the tea.'

With another smile, she left. Hadn't really achieved much, had she? Although it was nice to know that she wasn't the only one who thought Helena's behaviour peculiar.

She'd just finished the curtains in the main house and was ready to leave, when she had another visitor. John. She looked at him with such hatred that he flinched. She couldn't help it. Helena didn't love Beck. Carenza did.

'They belong together,' he said defensively.

'Do they?' she stated with feigned indifference as she shrugged into her coat.

'They love each other!'

'Don't justify yourself to me, John, do it to Beck.'

'He loves her. You were just...'

Snatching up her bag, she walked away. A diversion? Was that what he'd been going to say? No, she wouldn't believe that. Unlocking her car, she climbed in and drove off.

She didn't remember the journey home, just her thoughts. And it was all very well making grand gestures to Lisa, but what *was* she going to do? What she'd like to do was have a tantrum. And in a few more days the centre would be finished. She had two other jobs lined up, neither very large, and not until late summer; perhaps she should go home and see her parents, spend a few days of normality. Perhaps Beck would like to come with her. But

Beck wasn't in the mood to be asked when he arrived later that afternoon.

He let himself in, and then just stood and watched her, his face empty of expression.

'What?' she asked with a defiance she hadn't intended.

'John intercepted me when I came back from Horsham.'

'Did he?'

'Yes. He was upset. I didn't entirely understand his explanation, but the gist of it seems to be that it hadn't been his intention to make you cross, but that his first loyalty must be to Helena.'

Folding her arms across her ample chest, she watched him right back. 'And from which you assume…?' she queried irritatingly.

'That you argued about her.'

'No-o,' she denied slowly. 'He made a statement, and I—queried it.'

'And that's all you intend to say?'

'That's all I intend to say,' she agreed. 'Coffee?'

'Please.'

Turning away, she switched on the percolator and added casually, 'I met her today.'

'Yes, she said.'

'And what else did she say?'

When he didn't answer, she turned, and he gave her a bland smile.

'Fine.'

'Are any plates about to be broken?' he enquired casually.

'Nope. I only ever break other people's.'

'But you are in a temper?'

'Irritated, I think would be more accurate.' Taking his mug from the cupboard, she added the minuscule amount of milk that he took and poured in the coffee. Stirring it, she handed it to him.

'Thank you,' he said with grave courtesy. 'Are we having a row?'

'No.'

'Good.'

When he said nothing more, she leaned against the work surface and continued to survey him. 'Did you forget something?'

'I don't think so, why?'

'Oh, no reason,' she said airily, 'just that I was expecting a little homily on not interfering.'

'I never give homilies.'

'How unpredictable of you.'

His lips twitched. Hers didn't.

'I also saw Lisa,' she announced. 'I liked her.'

'So do I.'

'She said Helena was twenty-eight.'

'So I believe.'

Levering herself slowly upright, she sauntered past him. 'Find out what lotion she uses, will you? I do feel such magic should be shared with the rest of the world.'

She heard him laugh. Refusing to be amused, she

walked into the lounge and threw herself into the armchair.

'John said you used to be contentious,' she added loudly as she idly flipped through a magazine that had come through the door.

'I would start a discussion sometimes just to make people think for themselves,' he explained as he walked in to join her. 'I'm not sure it was contentious.'

She gave a little movement of her head to show she'd heard, then said equally casually, 'I'd also better tell you that I didn't like her.'

'Tell? Or warn?'

'I'm not sure.'

He tweaked the magazine out of her hand and tossed it on the floor. He then put his mug on the mantelpiece and crouched down in front of her.

'Stop it,' he reproved softly. There was a small lace of amusement in his eyes.

'I don't want to stop it. It's the mood I'm in. She acts like a child.'

'And that, my dear girl, is rather like the pot calling the kettle.'

Pursing her lips, she refused to look at him. 'Perhaps I should move into the house then we could have a nice little *ménage à trois*.'

'I don't think so,' he said drily. 'You'd make mincemeat of her.'

Looking at him, she tried to decide if he genuinely believed that, and decided that he did.

'Just what is it you're fighting for?' he asked gently.

'You.'

'But I'm already won.'

'Are you?' she asked sadly.

'Yes.'

'It doesn't feel like it.'

Gently dislodging her, he took her place and pulled her on to his lap. 'You're getting this out of all proportion. She's staying in the house for a few days; I barely even see her. I spend most of my time with you, but I won't ask her to leave, Carrie. She knows the situation, knows that I'm involved with you.'

Involved, but not in love. 'And she doesn't make advances?'

'No.'

'What did she say about me?'

'That she thought you seemed very nice.'

Astonished, she just looked at him. 'But big?'

'Big wasn't mentioned.' His lips quivered, and then he kissed her. She wished she felt comforted, but she didn't. How did you fight someone who said you were nice? Or the fact that the person she said it to believed them? And he did believe Helena. He also thought she was a nice person. And she wasn't. Carenza *knew* she wasn't.

'What happened to the man she was supposed to be with?'

'She said he was just a friend. And I really don't want to keep discussing Helena.'

There was a slight edge to his voice that she thought she had better take notice of. 'OK,' she agreed, and kissed him back.

Helena was still at the house a week later. The conference centre was finished, and Carrie couldn't *keep* rearranging pictures just to delay the inevitable. With one last, final look around just to make sure nothing had been forgotten, she collected her things and drove back to the flat. She didn't see Helena, or Lisa, or John.

'I thought I might take a couple of days off,' she told Beck when he arrived a few hours later. 'Go down and see my parents. Will you come?'

'I'd like that.'

'Really?' she asked, pleased.

'Yes, really. Monday and Tuesday will be best for me, come back Wednesday.'

She smiled at him. 'I'll give them a ring later. What did you think of the centre? Did you go and see?'

'Mm-hmm. I thought it was very nice. How much do I owe you?'

'A lot... Only *nice*?'

He laughed. 'You did a great job; you're a very clever girl, and I think it looks terrific. We already have a booking for the end of April.'

'Good.'

'And I thought I might close the restaurant for a month or two, take a break. We're booked up to the end of June, but I thought I might instruct Lisa not to take any more bookings until September. If you can fit it into your busy schedule, how about coming sailing with me?'

'Just the two of us?' she asked hopefully.

'Just the two of us.'

'Yes, please.' And for a little while it was all right. Until the Monday morning they were due to leave for Devon. When Helena rang to say she'd broken her ankle.

CHAPTER SEVEN

'YOU go on ahead; I'll join you as soon as I can—
I can't leave her, Carenza. John is at work this week,
Lisa has the twins; there isn't anyone else.'

'No, no, of course there isn't.' Masking her disappointment and her fear, she forced a smile. She
supposed Beck must have given Helena her number
in case of emergencies, but the thought of Helena
being alone with him, with herself out of the way...
'I'll come with you,' she announced abruptly.

He gave her a look of mocking reproof. 'I don't
think so.'

'Yes,' she argued determinedly. 'And anyway, if
she can't do much for herself, she might be glad of
another woman. Someone to help her to the bathroom, help her dress.'

'Help her depart?' he asked drily.

'I didn't say that.'

'You didn't have to, and if she needs help with
intimate things I can ask Lisa.'

'Lisa doesn't like her either.'

'Don't be ridiculous. You're getting this out of all
proportion, you know,' he reproved gently.

No, she wasn't.

'What on earth do you think can happen?'

'Knowing Helena,' she said gloomily, 'anything.'

'But you don't know her. Go to Devon.'

He kissed her, smiled at her. 'I'll see you when you get back. Wednesday?'

She nodded.

When he'd gone she stood where he had left her for long, long moments, her face thoughtful. What did she think could happen? She didn't know, but whatever it was it wouldn't be good. Not for her, anyway.

In which case... Snatching up her car keys, she grabbed her case and drove down to Beck's. What could he do? Evict her?

Parking behind his Land Rover, she took a deep breath as though she were going into battle. Which was exactly what it felt like.

They were both in the lounge. Beck was leaning against the fireplace, his back to her; Helena, one heavily bandaged ankle resting on a footstool, a pair of crutches beside her, was looking up at him.

'I am sorry. I've ruined all your plans.' She sounded genuine and sweet and gentle.

'It doesn't matter.'

'Of course it matters; I—'

'Who took you to the hospital?' he interrupted.

'I did,' she said proudly.

'A bit foolish, wasn't it?'

'But there was no one else to ask,' she said reasonably. 'And it is my left foot, so it was all right to drive.'

'And you got home the same way?'

'Yes, but then it started hurting and I discovered I couldn't *do* anything. I panicked. I'm sorry. But I'll be all right now. You go off to Devon.'

Watching this byplay, Carrie didn't know whether to laugh or applaud. 'Not broken, then?'

They both looked round, Beck with wry acceptance, Helena, after a swift flash of anger that she saw and Beck didn't, with a brilliant smile. 'Carenza!' she exclaimed as though it were the best thing to have happened to her all day. 'How nice.'

'Yes,' she agreed with the same false amity. 'How awful it would have been of me to go off to Devon and leave you here alone and in pain with just Beck for company.' She carefully avoided Beck's eyes. 'Just a sprain, is it?'

'Carrie,' Beck warned softly.

'It's all right,' Helena promised with a gentle smile, 'and I did rather exaggerate on the phone. As I was just saying, I panicked. I've never been incapacitated before, never...' She gave a helpless shrug, looked contrite. 'It was just so painful.'

'Yes, I imagine it was,' Carenza agreed as she turned away. 'I'll make some tea, shall I?'

'Helena only drinks coffee,' Beck said with a dryness that should have warned her.

'Then I'll make coffee,' she said brightly.

After filling the kettle, mouth slightly pursed, she put it carefully on the Aga.

'What are you doing here?' he asked softly from behind her.

'Helping.'

'Carrie…'

'But I am.' Turning, she smiled at him. He didn't smile back.

'It isn't going to work, you know.'

'Of course it is,' she said staunchly. 'She needs help; I'm here to make sure she gets it.'

'That's what worries me.'

'What hospital did she go to?'

'I have no idea. The one in Horsham, I imagine.'

'She should have called a cab. It's dangerous to drive with a bandaged foot.'

'I'll be sure to tell her.'

'Good. Does she take sugar?'

'Two, and plenty of milk; use the cafetière.'

'She doesn't like instant?' she asked sweetly.

'No. I'll have mine in the study.' Walking off, he left her to it.

'Coward,' she said softly.

She hadn't known he had a study. How hard could it be to find? Putting out cups, milk and sugar on a tray, she poured Beck's and went to find him. The study was in a room at the foot of the stairs. Carrying it in, she put it in front of him where he sat at a large desk. The rest of the room was rather spartan.

'Thank you,' he said with the same dryness.

'Pleasure.'

Walking out, she poured her own coffee and left it in the kitchen; she didn't imagine Helena would be expecting them to sit together and have a girlish chat.

'Perhaps I should get a little bell,' Helena murmured sweetly as Carrie put the tray down.

'Hang it round your neck, should we? Sorry,' she apologised insincerely, 'shouldn't give you ammunition, should I?'

'No. Pour the coffee, would you?'

'Certainly. Do you take hemlock?'

Helena smiled at her, the sweetest of sweet, sweet smiles. Accepting the coffee, she mused, 'I wonder if I underestimated you?'

'Don't even doubt it.'

'No, forewarned is forearmed, isn't it? But are you devious enough to keep him, I wonder?'

'Only time will tell,' Carrie returned flippantly. 'How long are you intending to be out of action for?'

She gave a helpless smile. Sweet and reproving. 'I do wish you'd go to Devon. I hate to think of you missing your holiday. Beck and I are just friends. He's entirely trustworthy, you know.'

'I do know...'

'Beck,' she continued gently as her gaze moved past Carrie, 'please persuade her to have her holiday.'

A look in her eyes that only Helena could see, she gave a humourless smile. Never stand with your back to the door, Carenza; you just never know who might be creeping up on you. Especially when your enemy can *see* who it is, and angle the conversation accordingly.

He gently took Carenza's arm and led her from the room. 'Devon.'

'No.'

'Yes.' Opening the back door, he ushered her out. '*Don't* you trust me, Carenza?'

'Yes.'

'Then go to Devon. I promise to lock my bedroom door each night.'

Standing in front of him, looking up into his face, she made one last plea. 'Beck…'

'Devon.'

Giving him a look of disgust, she turned away. 'You're playing right into her hands, you do know that, don't you?'

'No. Get in the car. I'll come and meet your parents another time.'

Climbing in, her face set, she gave him one last look. 'I don't think her ankle's sprained at all.'

'No, you wouldn't. I would have thought you more charitable than this. And why on earth would she lie? I *know* her, Carenza. You don't.'

But she did. She thought she knew her very well indeed. Holding the car door open, she blurted, 'John knew where she was all the time, and…'

'Now you're getting paranoid.'

'No! Listen! He did know. Ask him!' she pleaded.

'And if someone could do that—disappear, not even let her own father know where she was, let the police search for her...'

His face changed and she knew she'd gone too far. 'Go to Devon, Carenza.' His voice was flat, a little bit distasteful. Closing the door on her, he stepped back.

She'd never seen him look like that. So—disbelieving. As though he'd been mistaken in her.

After staring at him, her eyes wide and unhappy, she finally turned away and fired the ignition. How did you make a man see that he was being taken for a ride? And she hadn't meant to welch on John. Hadn't meant to do any of the things she'd done. Why was it, she wondered in disgust, that when she opened her mouth all the wrong things came out? And she *was* charitable—just not to Helena.

On the long drive to Devon, she had plenty of time to think over all that had happened. She'd been so confident talking to Lisa. Had even made a joke of it. Didn't seem so very funny now, though, did it? He thought he owed Helena a great deal, and he wasn't going to shrug her off just because she couldn't accept it, was he? But how much *did* he owe her?

Did second wives feel this way about ex-wives? And if they did, how did they cope with it? But then, how many ex-wives were like Helena? Why couldn't he *see* what she was like? She should have played Helena's game, but she wasn't like that. She had to sort things, get them settled; she couldn't *pretend*. And why should she have to? He must have known how she was feeling. He wasn't *stupid*. And now she'd left the field wide open for her. If only she felt secure in Beck's love. But she didn't. Didn't even know if he *did* love her. Certainly he'd never said so. And that was why she couldn't have it all out with him, have a row about it, clear the air, because if she did she had a horrible feeling she would lose him. And she didn't want to; it was as simple as that.

She quite hated herself for being so namby-pamby.

Pulling up outside her parents' house, feeling cross and miserable, she was in no mood for her mother's look of bewilderment. 'Oh, are you on your own?'

'Yes,' she agreed grumpily. Giving her mother a perfunctory kiss, she lugged her suitcase inside and up to her room. 'Where's Dad?'

'Somewhere around—in the garage, I expect.' Perching on the edge of the bed, she stared at her tall daughter. 'What happened?' she asked with fatalistic humour.

'I blew it.'

'Oh, dear.'

'He just hustled me out as though I were a package. As though I had no rights...'

'And do you?' her mother asked gently.

'I don't *know*,' she wailed. 'That's the trouble.'

Patting the mattress beside her, she urged, 'Come and tell me.'

Plonking herself down, in a rather muddled fashion, she began to explain. 'And that woman has more weapons in her armoury than I even knew were invented!' she complained bitterly. 'I don't suppose her ankle's sprained at all. I bet she drove to the chemist and bought herself some bandages, hired some crutches, and… She's two different *people*, Mum!' With a deep sigh, she admitted, 'I should have handled it differently.'

'Yes,' her mother agreed sympathetically. 'I expect he'll ring you.'

'He doesn't know the number.'

'Oh, I'm sure he can find it,' she offered soothingly.

'Not without the address, he won't.'

Her mother smiled. 'Tell me about him.'

And so she did. For the next hour she told her mother every little thing about him, all that he'd done, was…

'He sounds like a saint.'

'No,' she sighed. 'But I do love him.'

'Then don't let her win. Come on, come and have something to eat.'

Getting gloomily to her feet, she followed her mother downstairs, smiled at her father who was hovering in the kitchen, and gave him a kiss.

'I heard you arrive. Is everything all right?'

'No,' she denied despondently.

'Yes,' her mother contradicted. 'Or, it will be, and if you're thinking of sitting down at the table with those hands think again.'

He looked at his hands as though he'd never seen them before, gave a sheepish smile, and went to wash them. 'Didn't your young man come with you? I was sure your mother said he was.'

She saw her mother shake her head at him, and gave a reluctant smile.

Her father grinned back. A grin very much like his daughter's. Peas in a pod. Her mother was smaller, and slimmer, very much like her brother. She took after her father.

She did try to be cheerful, but she couldn't stop thinking about Beck and Helena, wondering what they were doing, saying to each other. Every moment alone, every lapse in conversation, her mind reverted to the house in Sussex.

'I think I'll go back,' she announced abruptly as she sat eating lunch with her mother the next day. Halfway to her feet, she added, 'I'll ring him.'

'No,' her mother denied. Putting a gentle hand on her daughter's arm, she restrained her. 'Ring him by all means, but don't go back to the house in Sussex. Go home. Let him know you're back, but don't mention Helena. Let him make his own judgements,' she cautioned. 'She'll trip herself up eventually.'

'Yes,' she agreed without conviction.

'But it isn't your nature to leave things, is it?' she

asked fatalistically. 'But just this once take my advice, darling. You'll serve no purpose except alienation if you try to confront him. He's obviously not a fool.'

'Only in this.'

'Then he'll learn in his own good time. People don't like being *told* Carenza. Even if he finds out you're right, he won't thank you for telling him.'

'No.'

'I know it's easy to be wise for others—' Breaking off, she gave a small laugh. 'As I'm being now.' With a gentle sigh, she added, 'Perhaps you're right. We're all masters of our own fate, or should be. Just because *I* wouldn't deal with it as you want to doesn't make me right. Just a worried mother who *thinks* she's always right.'

Carenza gave a small smile. 'He thinks he owes her,' she said sadly.

'Perhaps he does.'

'Yes, but I can't escape the feeling that she did it all for her own reasons, not his.'

'Or maybe she's just a woman who only likes men. Is it her having been pregnant that upsets you so?'

'I don't know. I could understand his loyalty, I think, if she were a nicer person. But she isn't. She's *weird*, Mother.'

'And you want to save him from himself?' she asked wryly.

Startled, Carrie just looked at her.

Her mother raised an eyebrow.

'Put like that…' she began, beginning to doubt her own judgement.

'Ignore her, darling,' her mother advised. 'Take what you have and let time resolve the rest.'

Staring at her mother, she envisioned a lifetime of ignoring Helena. But Beck had never mentioned a lifetime together, had he? Maybe he thought this was only transitory. 'Supposing she *never* goes away?'

'She will,' she comforted. 'This is so unlike you, Carenza.'

'I know, but I've never felt like this about anyone before.'

Trying to be helpful, her mother mused, 'Some women need a man to lean on. A *lot* of women,' she qualified. 'Maybe she feels threatened by you.'

She shook her head. 'Not this one.'

'But she might. This might be her way of dealing with it. She may not love him, but perhaps he makes her feel safe. Needs his strength for a while. Can't you be a little bit generous, darling?'

More or less what Beck had intimated. Instead of answering directly, she said, 'I wish you could meet her.' Forcing a smile, she added, 'Never mind, I expect I'll work it out.'

Lying in bed that night, thinking about all her mother had said, she determined to try and see it from Helena's point of view. And her mother had been right about one thing: if she persisted with this, she would end up alienating Beck.

Feeling more confident, positive, she rang him after breakfast the next morning. Helena answered. Determined to be polite, play Helena's game, she asked to speak to Beck.

'He isn't here,' she said sweetly, and put the phone down.

Counting to ten, she went for a walk with her father. She'd told Beck she would be going home today. He would be expecting her. Wanting to punish him, she had decided to stay until Friday, but if she did that she would only be punishing herself. She missed him. She would go home this afternoon, to her home, and ring him. If Helena answered, she would ring Lisa and ask her to give Beck a message.

She left immediately after lunch. Hugging her parents, promising to ring when she got home, promising to come back for a longer visit next time, she set off.

Just past Dorchester, the road divided. Left towards Salisbury and home, right towards Ringwood and Sussex. Not even thinking about it, she turned right. Telling herself she was being a fool didn't make any difference; she didn't turn round. She could always pick up the M3 towards London outside Southampton. If she wanted.

She reached Horsham at just gone seven. Sullen skies had given way to a cloudy night. No stars to be seen, no moon. She was tired, and just a little bit apprehensive. By half past, she was pulling up behind his Land Rover. The light in the lounge was on, the curtains drawn. She wondered if anyone had heard the car.

She quickly rang her mother on her mobile to tell her she was safely back, but not back where, and then she climbed quietly out and walked to the back door. Unable to see if the light was on in the kitchen without going round to look in the window, she hesitated. She didn't know whether to knock. With an impatient shake of her head, she turned the knob and walked in. Beck was sitting at the table. Alone.

He looked up, and then he smiled. Getting swiftly to his feet, he strode across to her and pulled her into his arms.

'I missed you,' he said softly.

So relieved, so overwhelmingly thankful that it seemed all right, she hugged him hard, rubbed her cheek against his shoulder like a kitten. 'I missed you too.' Looking up, she framed his face, stared into his eyes. 'I'm not staying, truly I'm not; I just needed to see you. I'll go home...'

'Shh.' Bending his head, he kissed her hard and long, and she kissed him back with all the yearning she had felt since she had left him two days before.

Glued together, exchanging hard, entirely satisfactory kisses, he finally moved his mouth from hers. 'Stay the night,' he ordered huskily.

'Can I?'

'Yes. We'll have an early night.'

She smiled at him, wound her arms even tighter around him. 'Very early?'

'Like now?'

Melting, loving him so much, she nodded. 'I'm sorry I made you cross. I can be very silly sometimes.'

'I forgive you.'

There was the soft tap of crutches that neither of them heard. Because they were entirely wrapped up in each other, it took Helena several moments of clearing her throat before they finally turned. Arms still round each other, Carenza's mouth swollen from his kisses, she forced a smile. 'Hello, Helena. How's the ankle?'

'Still a bit sore.'

'I'm sorry.'

'Yes.' Switching her attention to Beck, she smiled. 'You'll want to be alone. I'll make myself scarce.'

'Thank you,' he said warmly.

And Carenza held her tongue.

She limped out, and up the stairs, and Carrie returned her attention to Beck. He traced her mouth, her eyes, her cheeks with his fingers, and then he swiftly kissed her again, released her, and went to lock up, put the guard in front of the fire.

Returning to her, he captured her hand. 'Hungry?'

She shook her head.

'Thirsty?'

She gave a small smile. 'No.'

Tugging her towards the hall, he led her upstairs and into his room. Closing the door, he leaned back against it and pulled her back into his arms.

'Did you have a nice visit?'

'No,' she denied softly, her eyes on his face. 'I kept thinking about you. Mum and Dad said to say hello.'

'Hello back,' he murmured absently as he removed her sleeveless leather jerkin and dropped it on the floor. His eyes were darker, smokier, and she groaned, began to undo the thick shirt he wore. She felt—pliable. Running her hands over his bared chest, she gave a long shiver. 'I couldn't believe I could miss someone so much, miss this so much,' she murmured huskily as she began to trail her mouth across where her fingers had touched.

His arms tightened and then he put her away from him, tugged her jumper up and over her head and dropped it to join the jerkin. Eyes on her face, he lightly ran his fingertips over the flesh of her shoulders. 'I put the radiator on in here,' he informed her seriously. 'Just in case. I stayed in all afternoon, waiting. Ready to go at a moment's notice if you rang.'

'I rang this morning,' she said thickly as she began to undo his belt.

'I know. Helena said you got cut off.'

'Yes.' Helena could say what she liked. She no longer cared. Taking her by surprise, he scooped her up and sat her on the edge of the bed, then knelt to remove her boots. Tossing them aside, he began on her jeans. She stood so that he could take them down, and then remained standing, Beck on his knees, her hands on his shoulders.

Her voice barely audible, she whispered, 'I bought new underwear.'

He took a deep breath and looked up. 'It's very pretty, but it's coming off.'

'Yes.'

Hooking his fingers into the lace of her panties, he slowly drew them down. She stepped daintily out of them. He kissed her in that most intimate of places, then stood to remove her bra. Cupping her full breasts, he bent to kiss them and then stepped back to undress.

Naked, they slowly touched each other. Fingertips only to begin with, then palms, and then urgency and need. Toppling her backwards onto the bed, he began to make love to her with a skill that continually surprised her.

'I always knew you would be innovative,' she gasped.

'Depends on the subject matter,' he informed her almost shakily as his mouth continued to do the most incredible things to her body, her emotions, her mind. 'And you're a subject well worth the exploration. Dear God, you're beautiful.'

'A troll.'

He smiled. Working his way upwards from her feet, he gently massaged her, used his tongue to excite and arouse, not that she needed arousing any further. She could barely breathe as it was.

Combing her fingers through his thick hair, rubbing at all the sensitive spots on his scalp and nape, she pleaded raggedly, 'Can I join in now?'

He looked up, gave her such a beautiful smile that she felt a lump form in her throat. Wriggling down so that they were level, she wrapped her arms round him and held him as tight as she could. Staring into his beautiful eyes, she gave a shuddery sigh. 'I've never felt like this. I don't think I will ever get over feeling like this.'

'No,' he agreed gently.

She could feel him against her, all the warmth and strength, and desire flooded through her. Using her toes, her hands, she shaped him, felt him, traced every bone she could reach, every muscle until they were both quivering. Easing beneath him, she revelled in everything he did to her, everything she did to him, until they were exhausted and drowsy.

'And now I want to bath you,' he murmured against her ear. 'I have my own bathroom.'

'Do you?' The words were very hard to get out. She couldn't laugh about this, couldn't smile; it was all too intense and moreish.

'I can't stop touching you.'

'Nor I you.'

They kissed again, such a warm, gentle, exciting kiss that led to other things. Satiated, fulfilled, she nuzzled against him, felt her eyelids drooping and forced them open. But seconds later they were drooping again and he smiled. Snuggling her warmly against him, he pulled the duvet to cover them both.

'Go to sleep,' he ordered softly.

Feeling warm and loved, she gave a slow smile back and drifted into sleep.

When she woke, she was still wrapped warmly in his arms. His chin was stubbly, his lashes impossibly long and thick, his mouth serene.

Watching him, almost devouring him with her eyes, she slowly touched her fingers to his jaw and he instantly woke. His eyes were unfocused and she smiled.

'Good morning.'

He grunted, closed his eyes again, and she laughed. Rolling across him, elbows on his chest, she blew on his lashes.

He didn't open his eyes, but his arms came round her as he fitted her more comfortably against him. Arousal was swift.

Nibbling gently on his chin, loving the feel of him against her, she wriggled and he gave a soft groan.

'I'm going to make love to you,' she informed him softly.

A small dimple appeared on his cheek. His eyes were still closed.

Smiling, happy, all her troubles forgotten, she slipped slowly down his body. Touching, holding, massaging, using her mouth and hands, she turned his languor to nerve-quivering alertness.

And then they showered. Together. Laughing.

Wrapped in warm towels, they smiled at each other.

'I shall need clean underwear from my case,' she informed him hopefully.

'Which is in the car.'

'Mm,' she agreed.

'Which means I've been elected to go and get it.'

'Mm.'

He smiled. Grasping her wet hair with one strong hand, he kissed her. Slowly. Savouring it. When he finally released her, he padded into the bedroom to get dressed.

When he returned with her case, she was sitting on the edge of the bed trying to dry her hair with a towel. He dropped her case and took over the task.

'Helena would lend you a hairdryer.'

She smiled, shook her head. 'It will soon dry.'

'What would you like for breakfast?'

'Everything,' she laughed. 'I'm starving.'

Staring at her mobile face, he said quietly, 'I love it when you laugh.'

Sobering, she whispered, 'Do you?'

'Yes. I'd better go and get the breakfast before...' With a quirky smile, he turned and left.

She loved it when he laughed too, and there was suddenly such an ache inside her for—a continued fulfilment, she supposed. She had such an overwhelming *need* for this man. Was that how Helena felt too? It wouldn't hurt to *pretend* to be charitable, would it? She had so much. And perhaps her mother was right. Maybe Helena *did* feel threatened and that was why she was behaving as she was.

Quickly dressing, she went downstairs.

Helena was already there, and, remembering her vow, determined to at least try and meet her half-way, she said quietly, 'We're never going to be friends, so there's no point in pretending we are.' Aware without even looking that Beck had stiffened, she continued in the same pleasant voice, 'But we can at least be polite, show a semblance of—unity, can't we?'

'Oh, Carenza,' she laughed. 'How foolish you are. Of *course* we can; now for goodness' sake sit down. You like tea in the mornings, don't you?'

Hanging on to her resolve with a great deal of effort, because she *knew* Helena was only acting for Beck's benefit, she smiled and did so. 'How's the ankle this morning?'

Helena pulled a face. 'It's so *boring*,' she complained. 'I thought it would be better by now.'

'Which it should be. Didn't they X-ray it?'

She shook her head.

'Then they should have done. I mean, I know they're overworked and understaffed, but even so... I think you should go back.'

'Don't be silly. I'm sure it will be all right in a day or two.'

Looking dubious, Carrie absently accepted the breakfast Beck put in front of her. 'Thanks.'

He handed Helena hers, then seated himself. She answered questions about Devon that Helena put to her, smiled at Beck, deliberately touched her toes to his under the table, and when they'd finished and were getting up she saw Helena wince.

'That's it!' she said briskly. 'I'm ringing the hospital. You could have a broken *bone* in there!'

'Carenza!' she protested.

'No,' she argued. Walking across to the phone that hung by the back door, she asked Directory Enquiries for the number of Horsham Hospital, then hastily scribbled it down on the pad that dangled conveniently from a hook beside the phone.

'Beck!' Helena protested. 'For goodness' sake tell her to stop.'

'Waste of time,' he said unsympathetically. 'When Carenza gets the bit between her teeth, short of murder, *nothing* will stop her. Anyway, I happen to agree with her.'

'But I don't *need* to go to the hospital.'

Ignoring them both, Carenza spoke with the nurse at the Accident and Emergency Centre, and then frowned. 'Oh, right. But if I bring her in, could it be X-rayed? Thank you.'

Replacing the receiver, frown still in place, she asked Helena, 'Are you *sure* it was Horsham Hospital you went to? Only the nurse said that

Casualty was closed on Monday morning. All the patients were shipped elsewhere.'

'No, I'm *not* sure!' she snapped impatiently. 'I only know I don't need to go again!'

'Well, I think you do! You could be causing untold damage without getting it checked out properly. I expect that was what happened. Wherever you went they obviously had a double load, not only their own patients but those from Horsham as well. They were probably so busy they didn't have time to treat everyone properly. Didn't they tell you to go to your own GP if it didn't get any better?'

'No,' she denied mutinously.

'They should have done. I think one of us ought to drive you in. If Beck's busy, I can do it.'

'No,' she said adamantly. Shoving her crutches under her arms, she swung herself into the lounge and shut the door.

'Beck...'

'Leave it,' he said quietly. 'I'll talk to her later.'

With a little shrug, she left it—for at least two minutes. Moving the plates from the table to the sink, she murmured, 'She could end up crippled.'

'Carrie...'

'Well, she could! Where would the other hospital be? Crawley?'

'I don't know.' Taking the rinsed plates from her, he stacked them in the dishwasher.

'I'm trying to be responsible, Beck.'

'I know.'

Still frowning, still nagging away at it, she finally asked, 'Supposing she didn't go to a hospital at all?'

'Carrie...'

'No, listen! Supposing she didn't? Supposing she doctored herself?'

He slammed the dishwasher door shut. 'Carrie, Helena has sprained her ankle. I know you're Miss Do-Gooder of the century, that you overwhelm people willy-nilly with your devastating need to be right...'

'I do not!' she protested.

'No?' he argued. 'You didn't send one of your workmen home when you discovered that his wife was ill, despite the fact that he vehemently denied any need to go because his mother was looking after her?'

'His wife needed him.'

'No, she didn't. You didn't force the issue between us?'

'That was different!' she exclaimed in shock.

'No, it wasn't. You didn't go to see Lisa about Helena?' he persisted.

Silenced, she just stared at him. 'Lisa *told* you?'

'Yes. So can we please just leave things alone? Helena is not a child; if she thinks she needs an X-ray, *I* will take her.'

Temper simmering, she said with quiet intensity, 'Fine, but all I was *saying* was that if she didn't like or trust hospitals she maybe did her own *bandaging*.'

'No, what you were *saying* was that there is, in your opinion, nothing wrong with her ankle at *all*!'

'Perhaps there isn't. All right, all right.' She surrendered when his face darkened. 'She's your friend, not mine; perhaps I'd better just go home.'

'Perhaps you had.'

Temper taking over, she gave him a rigid smile. 'Should have taken my mother's advice, shouldn't I?'

'Which was?'

'To leave well alone and let things resolve themselves.'

'Wise woman. Pity her daughter doesn't take after her. I'll go and get your case.'

'So kind.' Mouth pursed, she followed him up the stairs. 'Of course, if you could hear the way Helena speaks to *me*.'

He didn't answer. He didn't need to; his back spoke volumes.

'And of course there *is* the possibility that she didn't sprain her ankle at all.'

'There is also the possibility that you won't leave here alive.' He didn't sound like a man making a joke. Shoving open the bedroom door, he surveyed the mess she'd left it in. 'Don't you put *anything* away?'

'No, I always leave it to the servants. Did you speak to John?' she demanded as he picked up the discarded towel and returned it to the bathroom.

'Yes,' he agreed shortly. 'He denies knowing where she was.'

'Well, there you are, then. Carenza tells lies, Carenza makes thing up, Carenza is an all-round uncharitable person. I can't *imagine* why you've put up with me all these weeks.'

'Neither can I.' Shoving her discarded things into her case he turned to look at her. 'Anything else?'

'No. I think I can honestly say that there is nothing else at all.'

He stared at her, his face hard. 'I might not have any family left, but I do have friends, Carenza, and if you can't accept that I might have debts accrued through those friendships, that I have other commitments, other obligations...'

'That I am not the sum total of your universe,' she put in pithily.

'Yes.'

'Then?'

'Then there is nothing more to say. I have no intention of jettisoning my friends just because you don't like them.'

'She's trying to split us up.'

'No, Carenza, you're the one doing that.'

With a grim smile, she asked, 'You really believe that, don't you?'

'I believe that you're jealous without needing to be. I believe that you're hurting and so I've been discounting half of what you say. She was carrying my child, Carenza...'

'And I can't compete with that, can I?'

'It is not a competition!' he said through his teeth.

'It feels like it. Are you sure it was yours?' she asked nastily. 'Sorry,' she apologised shamefacedly. 'I'm sorry. I didn't mean to say that.'

He turned away, a look of disgust on his face, and zipped up her case.

Hurrying across to him, she put one hand on his shoulder. 'I am sorry, I *didn't* mean to say it. I was cross.'

Straightening so that her hand dropped away, he stated coldly, 'But you did say it, which means that you thought it.' Picking up her case, he pushed past her and walked down the stairs with it. She heard him cross the kitchen and then open the back door.

Feeling ill, sick, wanting to kick something, and knowing that she only had herself to blame, she scooped up her handbag and hurried after him. She should have listened to her mother.

CHAPTER EIGHT

HELENA was waiting on the landing. All her weight deliberately on her bad ankle. 'Have a row, did you?'

'No,' Carenza denied stonily.

'Perhaps it's because you're fat.'

Disbelieving, disgusted, she shoved past her. 'I am not *fat*.'

'You are from the back.'

Abruptly halting, she turned to glare at her.

Helena smiled. 'Bye,' she said softly.

Teeth ground, Carenza walked down to the car. Beck was waiting for her.

'Your case is in the boot,' he said distantly.

'Thank you,' she answered in the same pithy voice. Hurting, knowing she was fighting a losing battle, but utterly refusing to back down, lie for the sake of their relationship, and remembering Helena's smug face on the landing, she said forcefully, 'She's using you. Are you really so blind that you can't see it? Destroying friendships. John, Lisa, me...'

'John and Lisa's problems are their own concern.'

'Should be,' she corrected, 'and would be if someone wasn't deliberately driving a wedge between them for her own amusement. I know you've known her a lot longer than me, I know you owe her a great deal, but why won't you at least *listen*? I don't lie, Beck.'

'I didn't say you lied,' he denied flatly. 'I said you were mistaken.' He held open the car door for her. 'Goodbye, Carenza.'

With an exasperated grunt of disgust, she said shortly, 'Let me know when you come to your senses.'

'No,' he said. 'It doesn't work like that.'

Brought up short, she stared at him in shock. 'What?' she whispered in disbelief. 'Are you saying that this is *goodbye*?'

'Yes.'

'Because of *Helena*?'

'Because you aren't the person I thought you were.' Turning, he walked back into the house.

Staring after him, her face white, eyes stunned, she took one step after him, hand held out, and then let it drop limply to her side. It was over? No, he wouldn't throw all that away just because she'd disparaged Helena. Would he?

Hurrying to the back door, she tried to thrust it open, and found that it wouldn't budge. Turning the handle this way and that, it still wouldn't open. He'd *locked* it? she thought blankly. He'd actually *locked* it? Hammering her fist on the door, she called his name, 'Beck!'

Nothing.

'You bastard,' she whispered. Turning away, she strode to her car, climbed in and slammed the door. Over-revving the engine, she drove away. Lisa was by the gatehouse trying to wave her down; she ignored her. Even Lisa had betrayed her. John she could understand, but not Lisa.

So it's over, she told herself staunchly as she drove home. End. Finis. And if he came, when he came, she would slam the door in his arrogant, disbelieving face. Had she lied? No. Had she cheated? No. She'd told the truth. She might not have been very *diplomatic*, but she hadn't lied. She'd tried to help him. And been accused of being pushy. And not very nice.

Slamming her hand on the wheel, a small snarl on her mouth, eyes hard, mind not even marginally on her driving, she reached her flat in a mood capable of taking on a tank.

There were several messages on her answering machine, two inviting tenders. She rang them, and went to see both potential clients that afternoon.

She took on both jobs. One was in Birmingham. A young couple who were down here staying with relatives and had seen some of her work. He was something to do with computer software, she was a lecturer. They would pay her hotel bills. They would like her to start immediately. Which suited her fine. The other job was local, and for which there was no hurry. She would be able to fit it in between her other commitments.

Temper and self-righteousness still riding her, she packed and locked up the flat. After snapping the deadbolt in place, which meant that Beck wouldn't be able to get in even if he came, she drove to Birmingham.

The house she was to decorate, and for which she had carte blanche—every designer's dream—was just outside the city in some very pretty countryside. The people were friendly, kind, and in any other circumstances she would have enjoyed herself enormously. But it wasn't any other circumstances. She felt betrayed and angry, stupid, and then lonely. Neither could she forget Helena's parting words. She was not *fat*, she assured herself endlessly, and she refused, utterly refused, to become self-conscious about her size. She was glorious, vital—big.

And if she played that last conversation with Beck over in her head once, she played it a thousand times. But she wouldn't ring him. No way would she ever beg a man to love her. Come back to her.

Throwing herself into her work, missing meals, barely sleeping, by the end of two weeks she looked very unlike the vibrant Carenza who had so captivated Beck. The couple she was working for were astonished at her energy, her dedication, and a little bit alarmed by her aggression. The local workmen were wary of her. She knew this, knew she was behaving like a very hard taskmaster, but she couldn't seem to help it. She needed to use up every minute of every day in order to keep thoughts of

Beck at bay. Not that it was working. She felt as
though she'd lost a great big chunk of herself.
Which she supposed she had when she looked in the
mirror. Alluring? she scoffed to herself. She looked
as alluring as a dead fish. And so she became even
more angry to combat it.

The next morning, scraping off wallpaper beside
the builders, who clearly thought she was mad, she
thought at first that she was hallucinating, hearing
Beck's voice where his voice couldn't possibly be.
Halting what she was doing, she listened intently,
and then walked slowly out of the house. He was
standing beside his Land Rover talking to one of the
builders.

He looked strained, and tired, and somehow rather
cross. He also looked magnificent, and really rather
commanding.

As though aware of her, he turned his head. Grey
eyes captured brown and wouldn't let them go. She
forced anger into her soul in order to maintain his
level gaze. How long they stood there like that she
didn't know. It felt like an eternity. The builder
walked across to her, removed the scraper from her
hand, gave her a little push in Beck's direction, and
went inside and shut the door.

She wasn't ready for this, she thought frantically.
Not ready to see him.

'What are you doing here?' she asked aloofly.

'Looking for you,' he said quietly. 'You look ter-
rible.'

'Thank you. How did you find me?' And, even more important, why had he wanted to?

'By telephoning every decorating shop in Croydon until I found the one you worked in. Your office door wasn't locked, and when the shop owner was busy with a customer I walked in and rifled through your diary.' He spoke with a sort of quiet simplicity. Almost as though they were strangers, but his eyes watched her carefully. 'Very, very carefully.'

'I see.'

'I put a note through your door, left messages on your answering machine...'

'I haven't checked it.'

'Not very professional.'

'No. What...?'

'Happens now?' he guessed. 'That rather depends on you. I know what I *want* to happen.'

Wrenching her eyes from his, her heart beating so fast she thought she might pass out, she stared fixedly at a weed in a pot. She had no idea what to say to him. She was aware of him moving nearer, aware of his quiet breathing, and she didn't know how she felt. Agitated, and hurting, and still angry with him, perhaps. 'She said I was fat.'

He halted, looked at her in confusion. 'Who did?'

'Helena.'

'But you aren't,' he denied gently.

'No. It's Friday,' she pronounced as though he might not know.

'Yes.'

'Shouldn't you be opening your restaurant?'

'I got an agency chef to cover for me.'

'Won't that harm your business?'

'I don't know. Is that why you've lost weight? Because of what Helena said?'

'No.'

'You haven't been eating?'

'I've been busy.'

'And now can't look at me?'

'Of course I can look at you!' she said forcefully, but she didn't.

'Can you leave for a little while? An hour or so? We could get some lunch.'

'I'm not hungry.'

He gave a deep sigh. 'Don't do this to me, Carrie. Please don't.'

'Do what?'

'Make me pay. Not like this. Not like Helena.'

'I'm not making you pay. I just… You said I was pushy.' Voice thickening, a lone tear escaped and rolled gently down her cheek.

'Oh, God.' Covering the last few inches between them, he gathered her into his arms. 'I was angry, disappointed that you weren't what I thought you were. There has been so much disappointment of late. Don't hate me.'

'I don't. Are you back?'

'I hope so.'

She gave a tiny little nod, a sniff, then raised her

head to look at him. 'I don't cry,' she informed him, almost daring him to disagree.

'No,' he agreed gently. 'Where are you staying?'

'Hotel, not far.'

'Come on.' After helping her into the Land Rover, he followed her directions, and walked with her up to her room.

'I'm not supposed to be here in the day.'

'I'm sure it will be all right.'

Halting, she said fiercely, 'Stop treating me like a wayward child!'

'Sorry. I'll ring down and ask them to send us up something to eat.'

Only vaguely listening as he ordered a meal, she stood in the middle of the room and wondered what on earth she was doing. He was back, but it wasn't going to be the same, was it? Things had been said that couldn't be unsaid, and maybe Helena would always be between them. Was she still in his house? She wanted him, had missed him so desperately, but was she willing to put up with anything at all because she needed him so badly? She'd flung herself headlong into an affair with him without thought, without *wanting* to think; now, perhaps it was time to be sensible.

With a twisted smile, she wondered how easy that was going to be. Just the thought of him, the sight of him, the knowledge that he was here, reduced her to incapacity.

When he replaced the receiver, she turned to

search his face. He looked tired, strained, and she longed to go to him, hold him, but forced herself to remain where she was.

'They'll send something up.'

She nodded. Aware of him as she had been aware of him since the first moment they had met, she wanted to run into his arms, be held, loved, and here she was, standing like a fool. With a weak laugh, she murmured, 'Do you know how many times I've imagined this moment? Well, not this precise moment; room service didn't seem to feature in it...'

'No,' he agreed. 'You think I haven't imagined it?'

'Have you?'

'Yes.'

He was finding it hard too, wasn't he? Because he couldn't forget his disappointment in her?

There was a knock at the door and Beck turned away to answer it. Taking the tray from the waiter, he tipped him, and put it on the little table between two armchairs. She walked across to sit in one, Beck took the other.

She wasn't really hungry, but forced herself to eat two sandwiches, then drank half of her tea.

'You look tired,' she pronounced quietly.

'I am. Tired, and heartsick, and feeling very— humble.' Staring at her thin face, he wanted her with a desperation that wouldn't go away, and wondered rather despairingly how many more relationships he was destined to cock up.

'What are you thinking?'

'Not thinking,' he denied, 'wondering how much of a fool one man could be in his lifetime.'

'And how much of a fool have you been?'

He gave a bitter smile. 'You wouldn't believe.'

'Try me.'

As though he couldn't bear to sit still, he shoved to his feet and walked across to the window, his back to the room.

Twisting so that she could see him, she waited. His accusation of her being pushy was still with her, and so she thought it might be best to listen to what he had to say, without interrupting, without explaining anything herself. Making declarations of undying love might not be what he wanted. He looked miserably unhappy, drained, but it might not be because of herself. When the silence went on too long, when he didn't say anything at all, she asked, 'How's Helena?'

'Gone.'

'She's better?'

He gave a bitter laugh. 'Better? There wasn't anything to be better from. You were right, you see, and I was wrong. I can be very stupid. But then you knew that.'

And she wasn't to be forgiven? Her mother had counselled her to be wise, to leave things alone, and she hadn't.

'I was angry with you because I was beginning to suspect that you were right.'

'And you didn't want me to be?'

'No, because that would have made me a fool. Did make me a fool. After you'd gone... After I'd sent you away,' he corrected, 'I wasn't...'

'You locked the door on me,' she accused.

'Yes. If I hadn't... If I hadn't,' he repeated emptily, 'I would have given in. The look on your face has been haunting me. But I needed to deal with you one at a time.'

'Deal?'

'Deal, confront, ask, talk... Never get between two women is my maxim. I was so damned tired of it all, Carenza. Of Helena, of John... I just wanted to get on with my life.' With a grim smile, he said, 'Helena doesn't like people getting on with their lives.'

She couldn't see his face, only his back, but the hurt that radiated from him was almost tangible.

'And then a man came.' With painful self-mockery, he derided, 'I have to admit that the timing in all of this has been superb. The baby wasn't mine,' he added shockingly.

The baby wasn't mine, she echoed silently in her head. 'Sorry?'

'The baby she lost wasn't mine,' he repeated. 'So you were right.'

'I didn't mean it,' she said quickly. Leaping to her feet, nearly knocking the table over in her haste, she hurried to his side. 'Dear God, Beck,' she whispered, one hand on his arm, 'I didn't mean it. I have a temper, you know that. Not a shouting, throwing kind of temper...'

'No, a deliberately dropping kind of temper.'

'Yes, I say things I don't mean sometimes. Not to deliberately wound, just—unthinking. And because I didn't like her, because I felt threatened, because she behaved to me as she never behaved to you I...' Feeling helpless and inadequate because she knew how much this was hurting him, she slowly forced him to face her. The anguish in his eyes was unbearable.

'All this time,' he said bleakly as his arms came round her. 'All this *bloody* time! Why on earth couldn't you have let someone know where you were?'

'It's only been two weeks...'

'And it hasn't felt like a lifetime?'

'Yes,' she agreed helplessly. 'Two lifetimes.' Sliding her arms round him, she laid her head against his shoulder.

'I didn't know where your parents lived, didn't know where your office was...'

'But you found it,' she soothed.

'Yes, I eventually found it.'

'I didn't want to be right, Beck,' she said earnestly. 'But she was so strange. She didn't speak to me the way she spoke to you. When you weren't around to hear...'

'I know. Lisa told me. She also told me John had known where she was all that time. Helena had begged him not to tell anyone, told him she needed some time on her own.'

'And he was in love with her.'

'A little bit, yes, I think so.'

'And he also felt guilty for deceiving you. You'd done all those things for him... Who was the man who came?'

'Her ex-lover. The real father of the baby.'

'Not the man she was with in Winchester?'

'Yes,' he agreed tiredly, 'the man she was with in Winchester.'

Frowning, she snapped her head up to look at him. 'She went *back* to him?'

'Yes.' Hands gently shaping her, roving over her back as though unable to help himself, he continued, 'His business had crashed, he'd lost all his money— and Helena didn't want someone who was destitute, especially when she was pregnant.'

'Did he know that she was...?'

'No. Not then. And then her brother died. Let me kiss you,' he said thickly.

With a little groan, her insides shaking, she raised her mouth to his and closed her eyes at the bliss of it, the hunger, the need. Holding herself close, as close as he was holding her, she kissed him and kissed him until she could no longer breathe.

As he kissed her, with urgency and desperation.

Finally lifting his head, he stared at her, his beautiful eyes sombre. 'I love you,' he said huskily. 'I wouldn't admit it, *couldn't* admit it...'

'In case you were wrong?' she asked gently.

'No, I don't think that was the reason. I *wanted* to love you, but so much has happened this last year, so much gone wrong, I think I was afraid to admit it. Tempt fate. And then it was too late. You'd gone. She didn't even like her brother,' he went on as though there had been no break in the conversation. 'Hadn't seen him for over four years, but his death was reported in the newspapers, and there was a picture of me. Team leader. Wealthy.'

'Good-looking.' Tracing his mouth, his eyebrows, she couldn't leave him alone. 'Really love me?'

'Really and truly,' he agreed as he kissed her again. 'It was all planned, Carenza. Not us— Helena,' he said confusedly, and then smiled at her. 'You're muddling me up.'

'I'm glad. Go on.'

'All planned,' he repeated. 'All executed. All believable.' And then he kissed her again, and again, a compulsion, a need. Mouth against her cheek, her chin, he grasped her long hair, held it tight in both hands. 'I had never thought myself a fool, gullible. I was so angry, Carenza. I don't think I have ever been so angry in my entire life as when she told me the child hadn't been mine.'

'I'm so sorry.' Beginning to see where all this was leading, she sensibly held her tongue. But Helena had taken advantage of him when he was grieving, injured, vulnerable, hadn't she? She didn't think she would ever forgive that.

Eyes holding eyes, a yearning in both of them, bodies as close as two bodies could get, she whispered distractedly, 'She's extraordinarily pretty. It's quite understandable that you would have an affair.'

He wrenched her back so suddenly that she nearly fell over.

'What?' she exclaimed, startled, worried. 'What?'

'We didn't have an *affair*! Where on earth did you get that idea from?'

'You.'

'I never said we had an affair.'

'No, you said…' Frowning, she tried to remember what he had said, and couldn't. 'You were going to marry her. Were living together…'

'In separate rooms. Carenza, we didn't have an affair. She came to my hotel room after I was discharged from the hospital; I told you.'

'Yes, but… Well, I assumed it all carried on from there.'

'Well, it didn't,' he said almost crossly. 'She came to my room crying and upset over her brother's death, and I held her, comforted her—' Breaking off, he closed his eyes in defeat. 'She *used* me! And I let myself be used.'

'Because you believed in her honesty and her grief. That's nothing to be ashamed of.'

'I'm not ashamed, I'm angry. She'd planned it *all*!' he exclaimed in disbelief that anyone could be so calculating. 'She was only a few weeks pregnant, but she needed to have intercourse with me as soon as possible so that she could say it was mine. She *told* me that! And she laughed,' he added in perplexity.

'Because you'd believed in her.'

'Yes. And I keep thinking, Supposing she hadn't lost it? What then? I would have *married* her!'

'Yes.'

'If Harvey hadn't come…'

'Who?'

'Harvey, her ex-lover, the man who came. She left him the way she left me. Twice.'

'Why did she come back to you?' she asked carefully. 'Not really because it was the anniversary of the baby's birth date?'

'No, John rang her, told her about you. She was hedging her bets, Carenza. Two men on a string until she decided which one to choose. If there hadn't been such an almighty row, none of this might have come out.'

'No. I wish I'd been there… For you,' she added quickly as his face changed. 'For you.'

'Sorry,' he murmured abstractedly. 'And then John walked in, and she turned on him like a wild cat.'

'How did…? I mean… Beck, I don't understand how all this happened. How did this Harvey find her? Did he know all along where she was?'

He shook his head. 'He was as stupid as I was. He loved her. The first time she left him—for me,' he added bitterly, 'he was unable to find her. He then set about working all the hours God sent to start up a new business, make enough money so that if she *did* come back he would be able to support her in the lifestyle she expected. He knew her faults and extravagances, or thought he did, yet still he loved her.'

'He was the man you saw her with in Winchester?'

'Yes.'

'And then John rang her to say you were interested in someone else…'

'And she couldn't have that, could she? She hadn't finished with me. Harvey began looking for her, tried all the telephone numbers she'd left at his apartment, and finally found John's. John told him where she was.'

'Without knowing the circumstances?'

'Yes. And then he got worried that he might have done the wrong thing, came over to explain to Helena, and walked in on our row. She forgot to limp. And all I could think was, Carenza's gone, and I'm left with…' Eyes snapping with remembered fury, he asked bitterly, 'How could I have been so *gullible*?'

'Because you believe in people, because you're honest, because you don't expect people to behave like that. I'm so sorry. You think it pleases me to have been right about her? It doesn't. I love you too much for that.'

'And I lost you because of it.'

'Temporarily misplaced,' she argued softly. Sliding her arms round him again, needing to feel him against her, she gave a sad smile. 'And so you rang round every DIY shop in Croydon.'

'Yes. I had no idea if you'd left for good, if something had happened to you, and when I did find you, looking so unlike your normal self...' He gave a small smile. 'You looked mutinous, and really rather magnificent, as though you could have taken on an angry horde. And won.'

'And for a moment you thought I was going to be like Helena, make you feel guilty. Punish you.'

'I don't know. I don't think I expected to be forgiven.'

'How can I not forgive you?' she asked softly. 'Stop beating yourself up.'

'I can't seem to stop. I keep going over it and over it, telling myself, trying to make myself believe that she deliberately sought me out at the hospital, not out of compassion, not out of grief for her brother, but deliberately. She had no love for me, no affection, didn't even care what sort of man I was. How can there be people like that?'

'I don't know.'

'I would never have said I was naive.'

'But you do have a rather old-fashioned view of women, don't you?' she asked gently.

'Do I?' he asked in surprise.

'I think so. Not chauvinistic, I don't mean, not kitchen-sink syndrome, but you expect them to be fair, honest, gentle, don't you?'

'No-o,' he denied slowly. 'I've met some very aggressive women…'

'I don't mean those,' she smiled, 'not the ones competing in a man's world, or what is supposedly a man's world. I mean the ones men think they might take home to mother. It still exists, doesn't it? That myth?'

Face thoughtful, he finally admitted, 'I don't know. With men's traditional role being eroded, women becoming more and more competitive, perhaps we do still hope for someone—gentle.'

'Wifely?'

His eyes smiled. 'Like Lisa? Earth mother?'

'Mm. And I can't believe she told you what I said!' she exclaimed sadly. 'I liked her, trusted her.'

'She didn't,' he confessed.

'What? But you said…'

'She told me you'd gone to see her. She didn't tell me why.'

'Beck!' she protested. 'I nearly ran her over!' she exaggerated.

'Sorry. I was angry. I didn't want Helena there; she used to drive me insane with her prattle… Stop smiling.'

'Sorry,' she apologised insincerely as her eyes continued to light up.

'And I suppose I felt guilty for wanting her to go away, for wanting to be with you all the time.'

'And then I began to seem a not very nice person. I *wish* I had left it all alone.'

'And if wishes were horses beggars would ride. I have a lot to apologise for, don't I?'

'No.'

'I thought I had found her, you see. The perfect partner. someone to laugh with, love with. A companion…' Letting out his breath on a deep sigh, he gave a crooked smile. 'Invincible?'

'You came through it.' Needing to know, afraid, almost, to ask, she queried hesitantly, 'Did you truly never feel that way about Helena?'

'No.'

'And did she…?'

'Want to sleep with me after that first time? Yes, but not because she thought me a terrific lover,' he mocked himself. 'I know now that it was because she wanted me on a string. I was supposed to fall in love with her; other men always had, or so she told me. But I wasn't in love with her. I wasn't even attracted to her. I didn't *dislike* her. I was grateful. I don't understand deviousness, why people can't say what they mean… Sorry. You did, didn't you? And I believed the wrong person.'

With a small smile, still rubbing her hand rhythmically up and down his broad chest, she asked, 'Why was John so sure that you adored each other?'

'Because she told him so. She could be very believable. *Was* very believable.'

Beginning to learn her lesson, she didn't make an assumption, but asked instead, 'Why did she leave without taking anything with her?'

'You know why, or at least suspect, don't you?'

'Tell me anyway.'

'She left because she was bored. But she left in such a way that she could come back if other options didn't work out. Amnesia, breakdown, whatever story she invented, she knew she would be believed. People always did believe her. She looked young, helpless, and she wanted to punish me.'

'For not loving her?'

'For not playing her game. I don't think she's capable of love, but she expected men to love her. *Needed* it, I think. So she went back to Harvey. She didn't want any of us to escape, you see. She'd heard that he was building a new life for himself, making money again... Little snares, little hooks...'

'Poor Harvey.'

'Yes, he was devastated when he found out about the baby. Utterly devastated.'

'Because he loved her.'

'Yes. And John looked as though he'd been hit with a brick. He doesn't understand deviousness either.'

'Neither does Lisa,' she pointed out more fairly. 'Has she forgiven him?'

'Not yet. And I don't want to talk about this.'

'But I need to know,' she said firmly. 'I do need to know. Please. It's important to me, Beck.'

He nodded.

'Has Helena gone back to Harvey?'

'No. He won't have her back, not now. Pain like that goes too deep. I don't know where she's gone. She took all her things, and then left. She wasn't even *embarrassed*!' he exclaimed in disbelief. 'She laughed, said all men were fools and easy to manipulate. Don't say it,' he warned.

She smiled. 'I wasn't going to.'

'How long is this job going to take?'

'Another month.' Sadness in her eyes, she whispered, 'I'm going to miss you.'

'I'm not going anywhere.'

Eyes widening, she asking hopefully, 'You aren't?'

'No.'

'But what about the restaurant?'

'I'll go home Friday mornings, and come back Sunday nights. I can see you in the evenings after work. See you in the mornings before you go.'

'And at night?'

'At night, you'll be in my arms. Won't you?'

'Yes.'

'I'm not letting you go, Carenza.'

'I don't want you to let me go.'

'And if I had never met her we could have been married by now.'

'Married?' she whispered in shock.

'Yes. Don't you want to marry me?'

'Yes,' she agreed dazedly. Sliding her hands back up his chest, she leaned against him. 'Make love to me.'

Holding her tight against him, he laid his face against her hair. 'I can't believe it's all over.'

'I'm just grateful it is. I've been so miserable.'

'So have I. Marry me soon.'

'Yes.'

He escorted her back to work, left her at the door. He smiled, and then kissed her. 'What time do you finish?'

'Five.'

'Then I'll see you in our room at five past.' He opened the door for her and gave her a little push, much as the builder had done earlier.

No one was working. As she entered, they all looked at her, and slowly, one by one, they smiled.

She gave a sheepish smile back. 'I'm sorry. I didn't think he loved me any more.'

'And now you know he does?' one of them asked.

'Yes. Now I know he does.'

'Good. Here's your scraper.'

She laughed and threw it in the air. 'Bosses don't scrape. Bosses devise.'

'Tell that to your lover.'

'I will. Be very sure that I will,' she said softly. She couldn't stop smiling.

EPILOGUE

SIX weeks later, fulfilling a childhood dream of Carenza's, they were married in the beautiful Georgian mansion near to her parents' home. Neither had wanted a big wedding, just immediate family and close friends. Beck had flown her brother over from New Zealand and was paying for everyone to stay overnight in a local hotel.

Dressed in a long dark cream dress encrusted with heavy embroidery and pearls, an extraordinarily extravagant hat hiding her piled-up dark hair, she stood at the open French door that overlooked the walled garden, and smiled. Beck was standing on the lawn, a twin on each arm. She couldn't hear what he was saying to them, but whatever it was they both gave a solemn nod. He looked up then, and there was so much happiness on his face that she felt a lump form in her throat. There was a sniff from beside her, and she quickly turned her head.

'Sorry,' her mother apologised, 'but I don't think I have ever seen a groom look so blissfully happy on his wedding day. No nerves, no anxiety, just pure happiness.'

'And that makes you sad?' Carenza teased gently.

'No, happy. You're so in love, aren't you? Both of you.'

'Yes.'

'So right for each other. I feel all full up.'

'So do I.'

Returning her attention to the garden, she watched Beck put the twins down. He remained crouched for a moment, obviously adding something to what he had just said, and they grinned and ran off to where their parents were standing, holding hands. It was nice to see that John and Lisa had resolved their differences. Then Carrie's heart began to thud with slow, heavy beats as Beck walked towards her. Tall and commanding, graceful and devastating—she thought she might burst with love for this man. Her husband, her lover, her friend.

He was momentarily waylaid by her friend Sarah who asked him roguishly, 'Got any brothers?'

He gave a small smile and shook his head.

'Cousins?' she asked hopefully.

'No, I'm a one-off.'

'That's what I was afraid of. If you get tired of Carenza…'

'I won't get tired of her.'

'No,' she agreed with mournful mockery, 'people don't. I love her too.' She turned, grinned at Carenza, and went to flirt with someone else.

Eyes holding hers, he climbed the remaining few steps, and stood in front of her.

'Hello,' he greeted softly.

'Hello.'

He held out his hands and she put her own into them. 'You look like an Edwardian lady. Beautiful, mysterious, and elegant.'

'Thank you. It's been a beautiful day,' she said gratefully.

'Yes, it has. I like your family.'

'They like you too.' He must be missing his own parents so much, especially today, but she thought it would be kinder not to say anything. Stating the obvious could sometimes be hurtful.

'Time to go?' he asked softly.

She nodded.

He squeezed her hands, and they went to say their goodbyes. She hugged her brother, her friends, and Beck went round shaking hands. The twins followed him like little shadows. Jessica was now sporting a flower behind one ear to match the one her brother wore in his buttonhole. Carenza grinned at them. They grinned happily back. Catching Lisa's eye, she smiled at her. 'All right?' she mouthed, and Lisa nodded. She hadn't really had a chance to talk with her before the wedding. On her return from Birmingham, she had been so busy getting ready for today, she'd had little time for anything else.

When they finally reached her parents, her mother stared at them both for long moments, and then she said hesitantly to Beck, 'We can't take the place of your own family, we would only ever be second best, but we would like it very much if you would—'

'Thank you,' he broke in, making it easier for her, and perhaps for himself. 'I can't tell you how much that means to me.' Gently taking her shoulders, he gave her a warm smile. 'I would give you a kiss, or a hug, but I fear to crush that splendid hat you're wearing.'

With an infectious laugh, she whipped off her hat, and hugged him. He hugged her back. Turning to her father, he shook hands with him. 'I'll take very good care of her.'

'I know you will.' Looking at his beautiful daughter, he smiled at her, then hugged her tight. 'I won't wish you happy, because I know that you will be. He's a good man.'

'I know,' she agreed a little tearfully.

'Go on, off you go,' he said with a roughness that he hoped hid his emotion. God, he loved that girl.

Blinking rapidly, she groped for Beck's hand and went out with him to the car waiting to take them back to her parents' house so that she could change.

'I'm not crying,' she informed him as they settled in the back of the car.

'I know,' he agreed gently as he wiped away a lone tear with his finger.

'An emotional day,' she said huskily.

'Yes.'

'What were you saying to the twins?' she asked curiously.

He smiled. 'Merely thanking them for coming to our wedding, and for being so good.'

'They're adorable, aren't they?'

'Yes. And here we are.'

With a funny little feeling in her tummy, she took his hand again as he helped her out. 'It feels different,' she said with a quirky smile. 'Odd, that.'

'It isn't odd at all,' he denied as he opened the front door of the house for her and then closed it behind him. 'It's a new beginning, a new adventure.' Standing close together in the shadowy hallway, he looked down at her, his face serious. 'I want to remember you like this. Remember everything about today. My wife,' he added. Eyes suddenly crinkling, he touched a finger to the brim of her hat. 'It's exquisite, but I can't kiss you, and I want to. Very badly.'

Hands trembling, she removed the lethal-looking pin, took off the hat, jammed the pin back in, and then sailed the exquisite confection down the hallway without a thought for any damage she might do to it. Shaking out her hair, she touched her palms to his lapels. 'Better?'

'Better,' he agreed as he lowered his head to slowly, and very comprehensively, kiss her. Voice a little breathless, he said seriously, 'I love you.'

'I love you too.' Tracing his face with her fingertips, her eyes on his, wanting him with an intensity that never faded, she asked huskily, 'How much time do we have?'

'Not enough,' he said regretfully. 'The plane takes off in less than an hour.'

'The private plane,' she agreed with a little thrill of anticipation. 'Taking us to Paris.'

'And tomorrow we fly to New York for some very serious shopping. And then Bermuda.'

She gave a slow smile. 'I like being spoilt.'

'I like it too.'

'But I don't know how to spoil you.'

'Oh, I think you do,' he murmured, his eyes alight with sudden laughter. 'I think you know exactly how to spoil me.'

Feeling loved and warm and excited, she gave him a quick kiss. 'Come and help me change.'

'My pleasure.'

Slowly climbing the stairs, hands linked, they smiled warmly at each other. Then laughed.

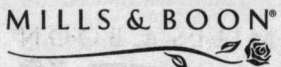

MILLS & BOON®

Makes
any time
special

Enjoy a romantic novel from
Mills & Boon®

Presents™ Enchanted™ Temptation®

Historical Romance™ Medical Romance™

MILLS & BOON®

Next Month's Romance Titles

♡

Each month you can choose from a wide variety of romance novels from Mills & Boon®. Below are the new titles to look out for next month from the Presents...™ and Enchanted™ series.

Presents...™

THE MISTRESS BRIDE	Michelle Reid
THE BLACKMAILED BRIDEGROOM	Miranda Lee
A HUSBAND OF CONVENIENCE	Jacqueline Baird
THE BABY CLAIM	Catherine George
THE MOTHER OF HIS CHILD	Sandra Field
A MARRIAGE ON PAPER	Kathryn Ross
DANGEROUS GAME	Margaret Mayo
SWEET BRIDE OF REVENGE	Suzanne Carey

Enchanted™

SHOTGUN BRIDEGROOM	Day Leclaire
FARELLI'S WIFE	Lucy Gordon
UNDERCOVER FIANCÉE	Rebecca Winters
MARRIED FOR A MONTH	Jessica Hart
HER OWN PRINCE CHARMING	Eva Rutland
BACHELOR COWBOY	Patricia Knoll
BIG BAD DAD	Christie Ridgway
WEDDING DAY BABY	Moyra Tarling

On sale from 2nd July 1999

H1 9906

Available at most branches of WH Smith, Tesco, Asda, Martins, Borders, Easons, Volume One/James Thin and most good paperback bookshops

FREE

4 BOOKS
AND A SURPRISE GIFT!

We would like to take this opportunity to thank you for reading this Mills & Boon® book by offering you the chance to take FOUR more specially selected titles from the Enchanted™ series absolutely FREE! We're also making this offer to introduce you to the benefits of the Reader Service™—

★ FREE home delivery
★ FREE monthly Newsletter
★ FREE gifts and competitions
★ Exclusive Reader Service discounts
★ Books available before they're in the shops

Accepting these FREE books and gift places you under no obligation to buy; you may cancel at any time, even after receiving your free shipment. Simply complete your details below and return the entire page to the address below. **You don't even need a stamp!**

YES! Please send me 4 free Enchanted books and a surprise gift. I understand that unless you hear from me, I will receive 6 superb new titles every month for just £2.40 each, postage and packing free. I am under no obligation to purchase any books and may cancel my subscription at any time. The free books and gift will be mine to keep in any case.

N9EC

Ms/Mrs/Miss/Mr ....Initials ....
BLOCK CAPITALS PLEASE

Surname...

Address...

....

....Postcode ....

Send this whole page to:
THE READER SERVICE, FREEPOST CN81, CROYDON, CR9 3WZ
(Eire readers please send coupon to: P.O. BOX 4546, DUBLIN 24.)

THE
Regency
COLLECTION

Where rogues find romance

**Look out for the third volume in this limited
collection of Regency Romances from
Mills & Boon® in July.**

Featuring:

Dear Lady Disdain
by Paula Marshall

and

An Angel's Touch
by Elizabeth Bailey

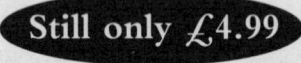

Still only £4.99

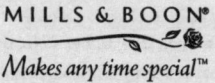

MILLS & BOON®

Makes any time special™

***Available at most branches of WH Smith, Tesco, Martins,
Borders, Easons, Volume One / James Thin
and most good paperback bookshops***